LOVE'S UNCHARTED TERRITORY

IKE MORAH

authorHOUSE®

AuthorHouse™
1663 Liberty Drive
Bloomington, IN 47403
www.authorhouse.com
Phone: 1-800-839-8640

Published by AuthorHouse   11/06/2014

ISBN: 978-1-4969-5178-6 (sc)
ISBN: 978-1-4969-5177-9 (e)

TABLE OF CONTENTS

Introduction.. 1

Junior Secondary School 7

The Practicals... 27

The Valentine Card.. 38

The Public Holidays..61

Bitter Encounters 77

The Reunion 91

INTRODUCTION

Who knows?
Who knows what the mind is capable of?
Who knows what love could do?

Love is like a tiny seed that germinates after many seeds have been scattered by a sower without any definite plan as to where it must land. Those seeds that fall on poor soil will never do well, while those than land on rocks will never germinate at all. Those that manage to fall on fertile soil where they are watered and nurtured by nature, truth and trust in this case, will germinate grow unhindered and eventually blossom.

These lucky ones will grow and rise to overcome, overwhelm as well as overshadow all obstacles on their path. They will be able to overcome and conquer everything.

Our mighty men of fame; warriors, heroes and scientists; have so far managed to conquer all seeming barriers in virtually all aspects of our earthly existence, including outer space and various other fields of human endeavor. They have however pathetically failed to make any significant dent on love. Instead, it is love that has always managed to rear her head, be that lovely or ugly, to conquer them.

Whenever falsehood, mistrust and suspicion, amongst other factors, come in to feed and fuel this all-conquering phenomenon, it manages to rear her ugly head. It begins to and dies, like the tender but large tree to plant-killing chemicals. It withers and may die. This could therefore fall and maybe destroy all in its path. Love could therefore die and then generate all those her untoward and destructive forces such as hatred, violence and destruction.

Love could therefore, though desirable, satisfying, recommended and nourishing, eventually lead to destruction if it is not properly tended. This presents that dilemma of love. This also points to that infinite probabilities as well as possibilities within its – LOVES – UNCHARTED TERRITORY.

We will soon come to see how true this could be.

"Please tell me that you love me." Cynthia had told Thomas.

"I love you Cynthia." That was the reply that she got from Thomas and that was more than enough to get her excited and very happy.

Who knows what he meant? That is if he meant anything at all. Thomas was a playboy; well at least at heart, and for that reason whatever he had in mind was very likely going to be different from what she will yearn for. She was as straight as a ruler, a straightforward girl who just wanted friendship, which could, if all goes well, advance into commitment. As for him, it was as of now just for the fun of it.

There was no way that she could know or even suspect that he was never all that sincere. This was because she had fallen head-over-heels for him, and it was at first sight. It was love at first sight. For him, he was just repeating what she asked him to say. In fact he did not even try to figure out or even to know what it all meant. It absolutely meant nothing to him. Fortunately or unfortunately, as the case may be for either of them, he was not yet aware of the fact that Cynthia was very rich. Had he known that, who knows what the mind is capable of doing, he would most likely propose to her just to get at the money? Who knows?

There are times in a man's life when he unconsciously, maybe also unknowingly changes – his character that is. His character would probably change without his being aware of it. At times it could be intentional but in the majority of cases, an external agent brings about the change. Both unseen and unforeseen hands influence it as well as many other known ones.

As regards Thomas, he was about to undergo a slow but steady transformation of which there was no way that he was going to be aware of. Cynthia was going to be the agent of change in his case. He did not know that yet and he would have disputed that fact if a seer had forecasted it. It is known that right from childhood, he had been a very deviant character.

Cynthia was the only child of an extremely wealthy businessman. He spent most of his time jetting around the world to attend to his numerous businesses. He had mansions all over and he lived in them as he moved around in his private jets. Cynthia was a particularly pampered child, having lost her mother at the tender age of four to breast cancer. That was why her father started his own foundation to sponsor research into breast cancer treatment. The foundation also helped upset the cost of treatment for most sufferers of this ailment.

To compensate for his perpetual absence he had left Cynthia with a fleet of three cars, each with a chauffeur.

She also had a couple of maids to help attend to any of her whims and caprices. Quite unexpectedly however and a little bit unimaginably too, she was not a spoilt child. One would have expected her to be one of those brats but she was not.

The reason for this unexpected character was because of her chief maid. Her father had employed this motherly figure to personally take care of her. She was called her governess though her real name was Sarah. Sarah was particularly kind hearted, a practicing Christian and she was relentlessly hardworking. These qualities rubbed off on Cynthia and that must have been the reason why she dedicatedly faced her education while living a fairly lonely life. She was more than studious when it came to her education and she was a very brilliant student who often blazed through two classes in a year. This nerd, if she could be considered that, was an absolute "A" student who had never missed a four point grade average.

Thomas on the other hand, was the son, an only child, of a Bishop and that was one of the reasons that Cynthia tended to have warmed up to him right from the beginning. She expected that as the son of a Bishop he was going to be very good mannered, which he was, as well as being a Christian at heart. She had her eyes on him right from the first time she saw him. Unfortunately though, he was about the worst of the worse when it came to moral issues.

Apart from that, he was not exactly a bright student. It was so unexpected, his moral character that is, that a professor emeritus of psychology and psychiatry was once employed to make a case study of him. The professor eventually came to the conclusion that the young boys character was a product of personal revolt, which could have been inadvertent.

His father, the Bishop, was a very strict disciplinarian as well as a no nonsense father. It was often claimed that the children of pastors were the worst amongst their peers when it came to moral standards. Many took this assumption as baseless, but this professor ended up proving that people were right on that assumption.

The path to the Lord is claimed to be narrow and harder to navigate than that to the devil or hell. Thomas, like Cynthia, was an only child. As an only child and male too, his mother really pampered him to the point of producing an irresponsibly spoilt brat. He was therefore closer to her than to his very strict father. The easier way was definitely more attractive to him and he never failed to show it and he always went for it, not minding his father's preaching and admonitions. Bishop Johnson, for that was his name, was such a perfect gentleman, as one man once put it, that even the devil can testify and vouch for him as to his Christian virtues.

Thomas, according to that professor emeritus, had that freewheeling mind that God had given to we humans, and he always put it to full use. His only problem was that he could not put it in check. It was as if his father always preached against one plucking that apple in the Garden of Eden, while Thomas was hell bent on plucking it. To him, it would surely be easier, more meaningful and more satisfying not just to keep looking at that apple but also to pluck it and eat it. It only made sense if one plucked and ate it rather than to remain hungry and blame it on fasting.

He was therefore very eager to get free of his father's corrections, the standards he preached and all those moral principles. That opportunity presented itself when he was spirited away into a boarding school. His mother was going to miss him and she protested. She wanted him to be a day student. He expected her pet to be on her side, but for once, he was on his father's side.

Thomas, according to that professor emeritus – Professor Lunamonga, had only done what was expected of a pastor's child. Their parents tend to overburden them with that idea of living a righteous life and bearing all those hardships and inconveniences that go with it. As soon as any of them is let out of that cage, he or she will simply fly away into apparent freedom. They will dive right into the fray of immorality. This, they believe, is what they had been missing all along, and that it was time for a sort of catch up.

Thomas's case was therefore more like the typical rule rather than an exception amongst them. He claimed that they all suffered from a condition which he aptly termed: *"Parent Triggered Revolt Condition,"* or PTRC. This case study actually earned that professor one of the most prestigious prizes in the field of combined Psychology and Psychiatry.

JUNIOR SECONDARY SCHOOL

It was in this school that Thomas met Cynthia. Saint Peter's Pentecostal Secondary School was located right in the middle of nowhere just to make sure that the students would not have any urban distractions and disturbances. It was located in the middle of a forest in the remote village of Petersburg.

On entering the gate into the school premises one would find himself in a very wide two hundred meters long dual carriageway that ended in a roundabout. Either side of the dual carriage way was lined, at ten-meter intervals, by tall rose trees. These were artificial tree trunks on which rose plants climb and some of them have been there for over five years. The entire road therefore smelt of roses.

The center of the dual carriage way was of many colorful flowerbeds, bordered in by well-trimmed hibiscus hedges. The roundabout where the road ended was right in front of a giant rotunda. This rotunda was topped by the school logo, which was a white dove diving down from the blues.

The rotunda had three floors. The ground floor together with part of the first floor contained their classrooms. The rest of the first floor was where they had their laboratories. The second floor housed the school library as well as their examination halls. The school faced due north. In each of the corners of the examination halls were elevated podia for the examiners. From there they could see all the students without having to move around. This design was conceived after they had visited the 'miracle academy'. This was a school where everyone passed. They passed mainly due to examination malpractices. In fact it got that name, miracle academy, from the rumors by other students that even a blind idiot can pass out of that school in flying colors.

On the western side were two buildings. The smaller one contained all the school as well as staff offices. The second, and bugger building, was the staff quarters. It contained thirty three-bedroom apartments with a central courtyard.

On the eastern side were two large hostels, one for the girls and the other for the boys.

On the southern side was a large one storied building. The ground floor was the dinning hall while the upper floor was the recreation room. Behind this dinning hall building was the sports arena with over three thousand seats and a lot of standing space. The entire compound was walled round. It was a very high wall topped by barbed wires.

From how the buildings were located, it meant that the teachers could look across from their balconies and have a full view of the hostel area, as well as every other relevant place in the school. This arrangement helped to keep the students in check.

For instance, it was easy for the hostel masters to see when light is where it should not be at night. The school had strictly enforced lights-out rules and the masters could tell when they are being violated though they had prefects to help enforce them. The juniors, students in their first two years in school, had to go to bed by nine at night. The bats, as they were called, who were the third and forth year students went to bed by ten at night, while the seniors went in by eleven.

This meant that by eleven at night there should be no light at all in the hostel areas. Sub-prefects appointed from amongst the bats supervised and enforced the lights-out rules for the juniors, while the seniors enforced their own. There was that instance when a final year student was caught fifteen minutes after the lights were to have gone out and he was punished for that. He was simply asked to go over to the recreation room where three teachers took turns to make sure that he never slept but read all through the night till seven in the morning. He was reading for an eight o'clock examination.

He went in for the examination and slept off on his desk. Of course he failed and that was enough to deter any other students from violating the lights-out rules.

The entire arrangement of the school premises was the main reason why it was considered a model secondary school.

There were actually three types of punishments meted out in the school. The first, and most common, was the runs. Here one is made to run a distance of one mile and back during the brake hour. He is ticked off in the school and then records his name in a register when he gets to the other end. It was the punishment of choice for less severe offences, but the accumulation of up to five runs in a week earned one the more severe punishment as well – the detention.

The detention is usually reserved for more severe offences, and while the run is done daily, the detention is done only once a week. One does his detention work when others are allowed off campus. Two detentions in a term earned one verbal warning from the principal of the school while three led to two months suspension from the school. Thomas managed to gross three detentions in his first five weeks in the school. Because of his fathers reputation he earned only verbal warnings for all three. For the detention, one had to do hard manual labor such as uprooting tree stumps or cutting grass. The work is selected so that it will take the offender at least four hours to complete.

The last was the instant punishment. The offender does the punishment right away and it is for trivial offences. The punishment might include such things as push-ups, kneeling down, standing at attention on a cupboard during sister and even the leapfrog.

Thomas had created a problem for Cynthia during one of his detention works. He was asked to polish and buff the entire wooden floor of the assembly hall. Cynthia was passing by when she saw him sweating away as he polished the floor, and she went in to ask him out of pity:

"Dear Thomas, is that not another detention?"

"Yes Cynthia, but it was not for any fault of mine."

"What happened?"

"It was that mathematics teacher again."

"What for?"

"I was crossing the assembly hall when two senior boys decided to molest me and so I escaped from them. I hopped over some chairs and landed at the other side just in front of the teacher. He simply punished me for jumping around the assembly hall like a monkey."

"Did he ask you why you did that?"

"I tried to explain but he asked me to shut up because he was punishing me for what his eyes had seen."

"But that's rather unfair."

"He had insisted that as an ex-military man, he had to obey before asking questions or maybe shoot before asking why."

"That sadist!"

"Tell me what I don't know."

"But people run across there all the time."

"Those boys even ran out by us as we stood there and he did not even as much as bash an eyelid."

"But this punishment is too much for that offence."

"Well, there is nothing one can do. I just have to go along with it."

"Let me help you."

"No. If you are caught helping me it would be another offence."

"I would prefer that to leaving you to do this alone."

"Okay then. Try helping with the buffing."

"Okidoki."

Cynthia had not yet started to help. As soon as she took up the buffing cloth, that same mathematics teacher came passing by:

"What the heck?" he shouted, "what do you think that you are doing there?"

"I am helping him with the floor."

"But that's an offence on its own."

"Why?"

"Because here we include it with abating the offender."

"But he did not do anything wrong in the first instance. Anyway one cannot abet a punishment."

"I can see that you are only trying to be smart with me. Just wait and see. Are you not Cynthia?"

"Yes sir."

"Cynthia Rodriguez?"

"Yes sir."

With that he stormed away. The following Saturday Cynthia was called up for detention for helping an offender do his punishment. Unfortunately, Thomas could not reciprocate as he wished to do because she was given some chores within the girls hostel. It was an area that was out of bounds to the boys.

Saint Peters, as the name implies, gives an idea of what the ideals of the school could be. It was on the day of Pentecost that the Holy Ghost came down onto the disciples. Peter was their leader. The school therefore had it as a rule that they had to always pray to the Holy Ghost to guide them in everything that they did, both teachers and students alike, It was therefore a school that was sort of dedicated to the Holy Ghost and the students in general, were for this reason, practicing Christians. They prayed three times a day for the outpouring of this spirit on them, and for many of them, it was this Holy Spirit that directed their activities and indeed their very existence.

The teaching staff of the school was handpicked. The Principal, Bishop St Claire was the born again Bishop of the Solis Rock Evangelical Church, while his Vice was from the Congregation of all the Saints Church. Both churches were renowned for their near fanatical stands on Christianity.

The other teachers in the school included mainly individuals from various Pentecostal churches. The Chaplain of the school was Anglican, but the post was, at the time they entered the school, vacant. This was because it was discovered that the Chaplain was gay and he was actually married to another man. No one was sure of what they were referred to as. Some said they were husband and wife since they were actually wedded in the Anglican Church, some referred to them as man and man, and yet others as man and partner. No one was sure of what the terminology should be but the students referred to them as the pair, or simply as mates.

There were a few other teachers that were Lutherans, Methodists, Baptists, Presbyterians and Roman Catholics. This potpourri of beliefs amongst the staff helped to showcase the school as not being religiously biased when it came to the issue of sects. Some said that they were hired on quota basis. One advantage of this mixture was that each sect strived to live a life that would highlight the fact that they were the best.

The government ran the school though the National Christian Council sponsored it. There was a time when the Satanist church wanted to be represented in the staff, and when their request was declined, they went to court. The government had reminded them that their belief was in Satan and not in the Christ whose believers sponsored the school.

The Satanist argument was that they believed in the Christ indirectly. Satan and Christ presented opposing sides and so one could not exist without the other. In fact the basis of belief in either of them is the existence of the other. One cannot therefore believe in one without believing in the other. The court had ruled that their argument lacked merit and could not hold any water since it was only seemingly and maybe technically correct. Apart from that, it was only an indirect and lesser belief.

Some of the students weighed in on the argument supporting the Satanists. They had insisted that, as students, they should be given enough alternatives to enable them exercise their God-given right to Freedom of Choice. The authorities simply ignored them and equated their argument as the theoretical product of that exercise of their right to Freedom of speech and that it did not contribute tangibly to the issue at hand.

Cynthia lived life that was not far from the ideals of the school while at home under the tutelage of her governess, and it was for this reason that her father sent her there. It was a school where she would feel at home. As for Thomas, his father was beginning to notice a couple of acts of indiscipline as well as deviancy from the usual Christian norms. It was for this reason that he sent him there to be straightened up.

Actually whilst most of the students prayed from their hearts, Thomas ended up with the very few that only prayed from their lips. According to him, he had already been steeped in more than enough prayers to last him two lifetimes.

Thomas was in fact completely mischievous at this stage. On their first day in school, he pretended to be a second-year student. He was going to play some pranks and enjoy himself with that act of hazing or cutting the tail as some called it.

The first new student that he came across suffered in his hands:

"Hey, young man!" Thomas had shouted after him. The boy heard this and turned towards him to find out what this "senior boy" wanted.

"Are you calling me sir?"

"Idiot! You don't address a fellow student as sir. Do I look like a teacher or a knight to you? Address us with please."

"I am sorry for that. Were you calling me please?"

"That's better. Yes I was calling you. Are you a fresh student?"

"Yes please."

"What stupid town did you come from?"

"From Abuja please." They had been warned that the most vicious students were likely going to be the second year students. It is not just that they would love to show off their newfound positions as old students, but some would like to retaliate for what had been done to them the previous year.

"Are you kidding me by saying that you are from Abuja?"

"No please."

"And by the way, why are you taller than I am?"

"Only God knows why please."

"Have you ever seen Him?"

"Seen who?"

"I hope you are not attempting to answer my question with another question of your own?"

"No please."

"In that case, have you ever seen Him?"

"No please."

"Have you ever heard Him speak?"

"No please."

"Then how did you know that He knows why you are taller than I am?"

"I don't really know."

"But you just said that He knows."

"Yes. That's because we were taught that He was all-knowing."

"You are at it again. How are you absolutely sure that He knows?"

"I have the faith in the fact that he is all-knowing."

"What of me?"

"Of you?"

"I thought you must have learnt something. Why do you like answering your seniors with questions? For your information, that is punishable."

"I am very sorry for that please."

"Okay. Do you have pen and paper with you there?"

"Yes please."

"Okay. Let's go over there where you can sit down so that you can write a letter for me. I am going to make you my scribe."

"Okay please." With that, they moved to where there was a desk. He sat down and Thomas started:

"Please write down the following:

Dear Miss Asterix,

I love you. I hope you realize that a man in love is like a blind fool, and that's what I feel as well as what I am. My heart sings at the thought of you.

In case I have other competitors, please ignore them and come over to me my love.

Dearest,

Collins.

"Excuse me please, is your name Collins as well?"

"Yes, and I have been wondering why you should be answering the same name as your senior. Anyway let's leave that issue for now. You will be punished for that later."

Later on, Thomas assembled a few boys that he met who he could trust and explained what he was up to. They were happy and joined him to a deserted area of the school. He then sent for the Collins. As soon as he arrived he started off:

"Come here Collins."

"Yes please."

"Kneel down here in font of me."

"Yes please." He then knelt down in front of him"

"Take a look at this letter and tell us whose writing it is."

"It looks like mine."

"Looks like, or is it yours?"

"It is mine."

"It was intercepted at the mail sorting office. Why were you trying to woo Asterix, my girl friend?"

"Me?"

"Yes you scoundrel."

"But I have never talked to any girl in that manner."

"Okay. Read that letter aloud to everyone here and do not say anything after that."

Collins read the letter aloud to them, complete with the ending that was: "Dearest, Collins."

"What is your name?"

"Collins."

"Please my fellow boys, do you see what this new boy has done. He has not even been fully enrolled in the school and he is already after a senior boys girl friend. He wants to snatch my girl from me!"

With that, he gave the boy a very hard conk on the head. The other four boys with him joined in and beat him up for chasing their gang leaders girl friend. He went back to the hostel completely humbled.

It was not until their first class two days later that he discovered that Thomas was a new boy in the school just like himself, but by then it was already too late. He regretted not having an opportunity to revenge. He had been conned by his own classmates. His only consolation was that saying that: "One's got to be a sucker once."

In another instance, Thomas had stopped a new girl that same period. This was done despite the fact that boys were not allowed to molest girls. He had greeted her:

"Hello small girl."

"Yes please." She answered in a rather small voice.

"What's your name?"

"Joyce."

"Joyce me?"

"No. Joyce Ike."

"I believe that you are a fresh student."

"Yes please."

"Face the other way and stop admiring me as if we are mates."

"Yes please." And she whirled around to turn sideways.

"Why haven't you made up your hair? Don't you know that you are supposed to be very neat here?"

"But I did make it up this morning please."

"Are you trying to say that I am lying?"

"No please."

"By the way, how old are you?"

"I am fourteen years old."

"And what is your phone number?"

It was at this juncture that a prefect came by. He looked at Thomas, but he could not place the face, and so he asked him:

"What's your name?"

"Thomas, please."

"You are a new student because I have never seen you before."

"Yes please."

On hearing that, the girl wheeled around to face him. It was then that it dawned on her that her classmate had been posing as a senior boy. She was annoyed for only an instant before she started laughing. All it meant was that this boy was only looking for a way to get her phone number.

The prefect only cautioned Thomas while laughing too. He was cautioned never to misrepresent himself again. It was both punishable and morally wrong, but he was going to let him go scot-free. Thomas thanked him for that and also apologized to Joyce.

It was not until after the third week in school that it all started. Cynthia, prior to now had never failed to notice this particularly handsome boy that had a near permanent half-smile on his baby-face. They were in the same class, and his name was Thomas. He was quiet and even looked like a gentleman, which he exactly wasn't. On his part, Thomas was always all eyes anytime he saw this particular beautiful and saintly looking girl who actually looked too pretty to be a true Christian.

On this fateful day they had come to the sports arena to watch a handball match. They had come to cheer their respective teams, and it was between the boys and the girls in the school. It was during this match that they, as spectators came across each other, or rather personally met for the first time. It appeared like a chance meeting, which it was not. Whenever she saw him, something seemed to stir within her but she did not yet know what it was and she actually prayed on occasions requesting the Holy Ghost to reveal to her what it was. It was not a bad feeling anyway. In fact it was a sort of beautiful satisfying feeling that often helped to trigger some faint adventurous curiosities within her. As for Thomas, he did not see how he could let her go.

Cynthia somehow or the other always managed to gravitate to somewhere not too far from where he was. As for Thomas, he always made efforts to make sure that there was no other boy standing between them. He had therefore edged close enough to her before trying to introduce himself to her for the first time.

Prior to the incident that follows, Thomas had always believed that whenever it came to chatting up the girls, he was the ultimate "guy." He had already come across a few girls before and it had never been a big deal.

Just as he was about to talk to her, he felt his heart try to leap into his mouth. It seemed to press hard on his vocal cord, which for that reason went numb. However he eventually managed to overcome that awkward feeling and situation, though his voice could only manage a loud whisper:

"Good morning." It came in a nearly shaky voice. Cynthia found it very funny because it was already four o'clock in the evening. She then glanced at her watch in such a way as to attract his attention to the time before replying:

"Good morning to you too." She had managed to suppress any laughter that reared its head, and sarcastically as it might sound, it came with a very calm smooth voice. That was the first time he heard her talk and her voice simply mesmerized him. It was that type of Angelic voice that could charm a sparrow off its flight path, not to talk of what it could do to a man's heart.

Glancing at her watch then, was to make him aware of the fact that it was already evening, but the only thing he noticed was her watch. It was an expensive Rolex watch and she must be from a rich family. It is not that he cared about wealth; his father was rich in his own rights. Most of these preachers nowadays tended to make a lot of money one way or the other. He did however realize his mistake and so he apologized in an even more shaky voice.

"I am sorry for saying good morning."

"That's alright, it happens." That was an unexpected and really mature reply. He had even expected her to act her age and laugh at him but she did not and yet they were each just about thirteen years old.

"Thanks for that."

"For what?"

"For your great understanding."

"Thanks too."

"I thought that you were going to laugh at me. Anyway my name is Thomas, Thomas Johnson."

"My name is Cynthia, Cynthia Rodriguez."

"Why Rodriguez?"

"What do you mean by that? What should it have been?"

"Okafor, or something like that."

"Why that?"

"Because I know that you are Ibo by tribe from right here in Nigeria."

"Is one not free to take up any name that he or she fancies?"

"Quite correct though am yet to see someone fancy the name Satan yet. Anyway I asked because I though that name might point to one being Spanish or something like that."

"You happen to be correct. My father was born when my grandfather, his father, was Nigeria's ambassador to Spain. He named him Rodriguez as his first name. As a businessman and an adult, he opted to have Rodriguez as his last name and his middle name as the first."

"Wow."

"I know."

"Rodriguez," he mused sort of thoughtfully. It could have been just for some effects.

"By the way why is your own surname not Nwafor instead of that Johnson?"

"Ha-ha-ha," he laughed, "you just want to get back at me."

"No. Not at all. Its just that the name would seem to be English and yet I know that you are Ibo too."

"Okay let me tell you. The reason is that my great grand father came back from England long ago. He was the son of an Ibo man that was enslaved during the slave trade and sold to one Mister Johnson whose name he acquired. When he returned to Nigeria, he decided to retain that name."

"That's history for you. By the way what does he do for a living?"

"He is a Bishop."

"For which church or denomination?"

"He is the Bishop of the Anglican Diocese of Akpom."

"I've heard of that diocese before. Is that not where the statue of the Virgin Mary cries?"

"No. It's the Roman Catholic Church there. It is claimed that her statue sheds tears whenever there is a disaster anywhere around the world. It is in front of the Saint Mary's Cathedral, which has a common boundary with the Anglican Cathedral where my father is."

"Does she really cry?"

"I believe that it does, though I am not an eye-witness to that."

"There is constantly one disaster or the other on a daily basis somewhere or the other. Does that mean that it is always crying?"

"My guess is that it has to be a major disaster."

"If God, according to one of his commandments, does not want us to have and bow down before graven images why should He give us signs and wonders through one?"

"Maybe it is the devil who could always appear as an Angel of light that is doing that. If the image is not exactly kosher to the Christian, then it might be a good enough reason for the devil to use it."

"That makes a lot of sense."

"Mind you God is unknowable and we can never fully understand Him. He could, in one of those his infinite and unfathomable ways decide to do that."

"Agreed."

Now that his heart was no longer in the mood to escape through his mouth, and they had got acquainted to each other, he was beginning to feel very bold. He therefore decided to change the topic:

"Cynthia, can I ask you something?"

"Sure, go ahead."

"Why are you so beautiful?"

She was taken aback by that curiously pregnant question. It was completely unexpected. She however blushed, but it was understandably unnoticed through her ebony black skin. She was indeed very beautiful, and it must be her type that had prompted that saying that "black is beautiful" and ultimately, "I am black and proud." She was stunningly beautiful with near Angelic smiles. No string of words would go any distance in describing how beautiful she was. In fact, it would be doing a disservice to her beauty to try and describe it at all. It would be injustice, and some might even regard it as sacrilege to try and describe this her beauty. Nothing will ever bring it into perspective. Its one of those cases of seeing is believing.

"Am I supposed to answer that?" She asked him.

"I hoped so."

"Why should I know? Am I my creator?" In fact it sounds like a silly question."

"It might sound silly to you, but I know why I asked that."

"Then why did you ask?"

"Because you look so beautiful that looking at you alone makes my imaginations run amuck. In fact I often forget what I wanted to think of not to talk of what I wanted to say."

There was a lull in the conversation as she paused to think that over. Only a perfect answer would do. She had to take her time because he also at times had the same influence on her. Finally she blotted out:

"I feel the same way too."

"You may not believe this, but the very first time that I set my eyes on you, my heart gave an uncontrollable flutter. It flirted with and soared in the wind like a butterfly to a gentle zephyr at dawn. My eyes looked at you, but it was my heart that saw you. Love at first sight, I guess, or something like that since I am not too sure of what it is. I have never experienced it before.

"Ha- ha- ha." She laughed as a coy smile that looked so enthralling that it could very easily charm an ape down from a ripe banana plant came over her face.

Thomas now beginning to brighten up with more confidence now returning. His heart had also finally decided to settle down in his chest cavity where it was supposed to have been in the first place. He was sure it would never try again to fly out, now that fear and anxiety were no longer there. Bristling with confidence, he now went on to ask her:

"Can I kiss you?"

With that, she turned to face him squarely with her eyes blazing as if with extreme anger. He was both afraid and embarrassed, but at that very moment the school bell tolled to save him. The referee had just blown the final whistle and the bell tolled at that very same moment. The match was over, but neither of them knew what the score was.

As the bell rang, it's sonorous and golden, though urgent sounds echoed and reverberated through the entire school compound. It meant that they had to hurry for they had just thirty minutes to wash up and be at the dinning hall for dinner. The bell had as it were, saved Thomas, and that was the first time that he ever appreciated that bell. He would always give gratitude to it. They parted ways in a hurry without as much as even one word from either of them.

They were surely in love with each other, but neither of them would yet fully admit it. Thomas was not sure of how she was going to react when he asked that question, neither was he sure of what she might do next. This in fact calls to mind the saying by a Love Guru that "if I say that I understand the ways of love, then I will be lying to myself." To put this in another way it would point to the fact that "LOVE is an UNCHARTED TERRITORY"

THE PRACTICALS

It was not until about four weeks later that they chanced to be together once more. Thomas had been making every possible effort to avoid her in order to save himself from any further embarrassments and her wrath. He still wanted her, but he was afraid of what might happen, of her reaction that is.

In fact the previous day he had missed his Sunday afternoon meal because of Cynthia. For this school, anyone that missed this meal would be considered as being mentally ill, and some would even consider missing it as being sacrilegious. It was the best meal of the entire week and they always looked forwards to it.

This was a meal that was different from the rest. It was fried rice with chicken and salad. Each student actually had the choice between vegetable or fruit salad and cold slaw. The chicken was always half of an entire chicken. It is fried, but was always soft, tender, well seasoned and invitingly juicy. In other words it was always extremely mouth watering. The students always came in early for this meal and would loiter around the dinning area till it was time to go in.

In contrast to this almighty meal was the Saturday afternoon meal. That meal was always black-eyed beans and yam. The boiled yam was usually very hard and some claim that it was dry, while the beans are usually half-heartedly boiled. It is never properly cooked.

Thomas was on his way to the Sunday lunch when he Suddenly saw Cynthia and her girlfriend Funke having some conversations by the side of the road while waiting for time to go into the dinning hall. He did not want her to see him and so he ran back to the hostel and hid behind his provision cupboard, afraid that she must have spotted him. Anyone who saw him, panicky and afraid, would think that he was hiding away from some terrorists or militants as the case may be.

He was that much afraid and so ashamed he was not in a hurry to see her. He believed that he had already stepped across that red line and there was nothing he could do to change that fact. It was like someone who had just released a very stinking fart while with people wishing that there could a way to unfart it, if there is any word like that.

They eventually met at their first Chemistry practical class. Everything was simple as if it was revision to Cynthia, but the rest of the class did not find it funny. Incidentally they were to perform the experiment in pairs and the teacher had paired Cynthia with Thomas. It was an extremely odd situation for Thomas as it was with virtually every other student, Thomas had no clue as to what the experiment was all about. Even if he had a clue as to what to do, it would not have helped since being paired with Cynthia would have made him so nervous as to go blank.

Each pair of students was given a small sealed vial. No clue was given and no apparatus was supplied. One was free to choose whatever he or she needed to identify what was in the vial. They were given thirty minutes to do so. They were brand new students and they were stunned because there was nothing in the vials. The teacher actually escaped from the laboratory so that they would not ask him any questions.

To them, one cannot analyze nothing, and most left too after the teacher had absconded, out of frustration. Thomas had to find a way out. He was not ready to embarrass himself and so he asked her to excuse him to go out and use the rest room. He never came back.

The teacher came back after thirty minutes only to find nine students left. These submitted their answer sheets. Four of the groups were smart kids who felt that it was a trick experiment and so they came up with the answer that it was nothing. The vial was a vacuum. It seemed like a smart answer, but they were all wrong. Only Cynthia got the correct answer.

Quite uncharacteristically, Cynthia decided to kill the break time by going down the flight of stairs through four floors rather than using the elevator. Right after the first flight of stairs she and Thomas nearly collided at one corner. Thomas used the stairs because no one ever used it and he wanted to keep away from you know whom. She immediately commented:

"I did not see you again."

He had never been so embarrassed in his life. Ashamed and confused, he stood there in front of her while trying to find his voice. He wished that an earthquake could occur there and then and he would gladly hope that it would suck him right into the bowels of the earth, never to be seen again. He however, some how or the other, managed to get his mouth to agree to speak again as his voice returned:

"I am very sorry Cynthia."

"What happened? I missed you."

It was only then that he resolved to hold the bull by the horn, no matter the outcome:

"Let me tell you the truth. I did not know where to start."

"But you should have just told me that."

"How could I?"

"Not even after how we feel about each other?"

It was this statement that brought him back to his senses. She was not after all so mad at him.

"You looked so worried and annoyed when we parted last time and I have been afraid to come across you ever since."

"Actually I was only marginally angry and it lasted but for a few seconds only."

"I was afraid."

"Afraid of what?"

"Of what you could do."

"But it could have only been words and words cannot kill."

"I am very sorry about what I asked for that day. I was only carried away and I did not know when or how I asked for that."

She did not want to continue with that line of conversation because she had missed him so much. She therefore decided to change the topic:

"I finished the experiment and submitted the answer sheet. We scored an "A".

"What?"

"Yes an "A".

For Thomas, it was the first "A" that he had ever scored in his life and he could not quite comprehend it.

"But how did you identify whatever it was?"

"It was a gas."

"A gas?"

"Yes, a gas, and it was very simple for that matter. It did not take even ten seconds to identify."

"I am all ears."

"Do you remember the gas we studied in the class the other day?"

"Which one?"

"The one that the teacher said is the commonest gas that we usually come across."

"Yes. It was something disulfide."

"Yes. Hydrogen disulfide, to be precise."

"Then how did you identify it?"

"By smell of course."

"By smell? What a fool I must be," he shouted. "Just open the vial and smell the gas."

"Of course. It is a colorless gas with the smell of rotten eggs. In fact he told us that when eggs rot, it is that gas that is formed and that's what we smell."

His dirty mind was once more working in overdrive. He thought for but only a moment before asking:

"Is it possible for us to meet once in a while so that you could brush me up academically?"

"In what subject?"

"All."

"Why all?"

"I am not sure that you are aware of my predicament. I am not academically sound, no matter which area or subject one thinks of."

"You can always come around anytime that we are free."

"Thank you very much. You have just made my day."

"Anytime."

As soon as she gave that reply, the bell tolled to announce the end of their lunch break. This time around, he was not happy with the bell as they dashed off to their next lecture. He did not want that meeting to end yet.

Cynthia had agreed to that arrangement because she knew of Thomas's handicap. To say that Thomas was not all that bright in the class would actually be an understatement. One of their teachers often referred to him as that dunce of the first order. Another one actually referred to him as a nincompoop.

The worst was in the field of mathematics which most of the students were not all that eager to dabble into. It was in this class that one hilarious incidence took place. This was not too long after they were introduced to Algebra.

Their last three lessons were spent learning how to balance quadratic equations. Most of the students did not like mathematics, as a subject while Algebra had been hated, and least of all that high-sounding section of it called quadratic equations. Many managed to cope with it, but Thomas gave up long before it was even started. At the end of the lessons, their teacher gave them just one question to test their understanding and knowledge of the subject matter. He gave them one simple equation to solve, to balance that is. Unknown to them, it was a trick question. It could never be balanced as worded.

The students sweated through the entire twenty-five minutes assigned to it. Most of the students secretly put their heads together to find a solution to it. Cynthia and Thomas alone were the ones who did not consult with others. Most of the class managed to balance the equation due to a few deductive reasonings here and there.

Cynthia's answer was that the equation needed one more factor to make balancing it possible. As for Thomas, he was so frustrated that he decided to throw politeness to the winds. His answer was: "Can't balance this. Do it if you can." The teacher did not believe his eyes when he saw that answer. To further increase the surprise, it was Thomas that submitted it. The teacher was initially confused till it struck him as to what had taken place. Thomas had never scored over ten percent in any mathematics class. In fact he once set a record by scoring minus fifteen percent.

Surprisingly, the teacher asked if anyone had a copy of the Holy Bible. Cynthia had one. He then asked her to read aloud to the entire class the book of Ezekiel, chapter thirty-seven, verse three and she did so:

"...Son of man, can these bones rise again? And I answered, O Lord God thou knowest."

Incidentally that was the prophet Ezekiel talking with God in the valley of bones. The bones of the dead had to rise up as soldiers to fight on his side. God had resurrected those bones to help them fight and defeat their enemies. Now the teacher asked the class:

"Sons of men, can Thomas rise again?"

The class echoed back in unison in answer to the teacher:

"O dear teacher thou knowest."

The teacher had suspected that a miracle had just taken place and that God must have had a hand in it. He had just made a mathematician out of Thomas. That was a wrong assumption. Apart from Cynthia Thomas was the only other person who could not balance it and he made it known, even if a little bit rudely.

Cynthia was not very happy with what had just taken place. It was not that she did not feel happy that Thomas had done well but because she had to be the person to read that passage which was meant to ridicule her Thomas.

Now that the groundwork had been laid for those lessons from Cynthia, Thomas began to feel that things were now beginning to shape up. It meant that from then henceforth he was going to see her more often. Unknown to him, she felt the same way too. She was beginning to often feel incomplete without seeing him. She was actually suffering in silence.

Incidentally Thomas was probably not so brilliant just because he was in every aspect his father's son. The Bishop, his father, only managed to make it in the religious section because it was the only area where he could make it and even then he was not in any way brilliant in that area. He only managed to scrape through elementary school and then managed to make it into a secondary school on quota basis. The school was situated in their town and the school was therefore mandated to leave three vacancies each year for the natives of that town. For this particular year there were only two candidates and so he was accepted even though he was not exactly qualified to get in. The hope was that he could always be weeded out with time.

On enrollment, he became one of the most toasted students. This was not because he was brilliant as could be assumed, but because he was so handsome that the girls always seemed to gravitate around wherever he was. The other boys, as would be expected therefore did the same too.

He was also outgoing and came to assume the role of being the hub of every social gathering in the school, especially parties.

Based on academics, he would have been expelled from school right away, but he knew how to get around the scores. He made very judicious use of any money that was sent to him, and his father was rich. Apart from his normal pocket allowance, he always managed to extort more money from his father on the grounds of having been robbed, loosing his wallet, paying for damaged school properties, buying new textbooks and more.

Luck was always on his side during these schemes mainly because his parents resided some five states away from the school and it was not always easy for them to investigate. During tests and examinations, he would pay those sitting next to him for them to allow him copy their answers. Whenever this was not enough, he would always go ahead and sort himself out with his teachers. These were usually in the form of money in exchange for marks. In fact when one of the averagely pretty girls wanted to pass a course, she consulted him because she was too afraid to talk to the lecturer. He arranged with the lecturer for both of them to pass and he would offer the girl to him. He arranged for those two to meet in a hotel room.

For their final exit external examinations, he managed to produce fake identity cards that let some of his teachers take the examinations for him. He passed out in flying colors and his parents were very proud of him.

He was a very calculating character and he was not sure of how it was going to work out for him in the university since he knew next to nothing. It was for this reason that he opted for the seminary. One other reason that he had for opting for the seminary was that, somehow or the other, he had always loved religious studies. In fact it was the only subject that he had ever scored as high as an "E" without any external help. Most importantly however, as a reason for opting for the seminary, is the fact that he had never heard of anyone dropping out of the seminary on the grounds of poor academic performance. In actual fact he had heard of a priest who was for all intents and purposes, a dunce.

In spite of his numerous adventures in that seminary, he eventually came out as a priest. The Bishop posted him to a small rather scanty parish in a very interior village after his ordination. "As luck would have it," he was rocketed through the ranks to that of a Bishop within three and half years. It was claimed that he was so good that it was spiritual intervention that elevated him to that post. Please do not try to ask me which spirit intervened on his behalf!

The hidden truth about his phenomenal progress had remained a secret. Two weeks after he assumed office, the Bishop visited his church for a Confirmation service. There were just two candidates for that, but it was at least better than none at all.

Just over a month later, the girl that attended to the Bishop during that his visit became pregnant. She confided on Pastor Johnson. She was a virgin and a very upright Christian and the boys and other men were afraid to talk to her. She was particularly pretty and a no-nonsense character. On that fateful day she was the person who personally attended to the Bishop in the guest room of the parsonage. She would always say no to any man, but when it came to the Bishop she was afraid and overwhelmed and that was when the deed was done.

Reverend Johnson immediately decided to capitalize on that potential scandal. He took the girl to the Bishop to explain what had happened. Within two weeks she was off to overseas to study nursing on scholarship from the diocese. Her parents, not being in the know as to what had actually happened, were very happy as she hurriedly travelled out. The truth remained a dead secret between Reverend Johnson and his Bishop.

Within three and half years, Reverend Johnson had risen through the ranks and he replaced the Bishop as he went into a three-month early retirement. Johnson went from acting for him to becoming a substantive Bishop.

Reverend, and now Bishop Johnson, was one of those preachers who would ask his flock to do as he said and not as he did. Incidentally he had more than a few skeletons in his closet, but I guess they had better be left alone. The only incident worth noting as of now is that his wife used to sing. She was a natural tenor and often sang solo in his church choir with the rest of the choir in the background. It was claimed that she had a voice that could bring down the angels. No one was sure of what happened or what led or did not lead to the other, except that they suddenly became husband and wife.

That was all about how Reverend Johnson rocketed through the ranks to become His Eminence, Bishop Johnson.

THE VALENTINE CARD

This quasi-relationship between Cynthia and Thomas had continued through the years, and they met with each other once in a while. For Thomas, having lessons with her was not his idea of one having quality time with his girlfriend, but there was nothing he could do about it. That was more than enough for Cynthia.

They however managed to stay together during their Christmas vacation, but not long after that, he was once more up to his usual antics. He had gone to a store and browsed through their valentine cards till he found one that he could send to her. The inscription on the front cover was: "Tell it as it is."

This front cover was orange in color with a purple heart right in the center. The inner front cover was white and with the same heart in the middle. The difference was that this time around, four Cherubs supported it. They supported it on their wings as they flew towards the upper part of the page, which looked like the sky. Then came the pink page with nothing on it. It was where the sender was expected to tell it a sit is. The inside back cover was white with only one word: "congratulations." The back cover was also orange like the front but with nothing but the logo of the manufacturer on it.

It took Thomas some time to realize that the pink page had a very faint inscription that can only be seen when held against the light. It read: "Mr. Valentino, tell her your feelings!" It took him an entire two days to pour out his heart to Cynthia on that pink page. It was in the form of two love poems:

TO CYNTHIA WITH LOVE:

PART 1
My heart ached as if stroke was apt to come,
My head ached as of hammer to the anvil,
My thoughts raced as though the devil was after them;
Then I braced myself to seek you out.

Nearer yet afar you seemed to me,
As I sought and searched in vain.
Nothing of you will ever fade,
For you're the one that's meant for me.

My heart seemed to run in chase of shadows,
Till it came to you my lovely love.
In glory and splendor yet unseen before,
There you stood as out from all.

I had ran, raced and chased around
Till destiny did bring you here to me.
I stood and moped at what I saw
As there you stood to quench my thirst.

My heart desires none and none but you
As I immerse myself in you,
For you have all it will ever take
To make my head swirl in recycled swoons.

Your looks alone like the early sun to me
Mild and mellow to behold and feel they are.
Tender and yet tenderer you seem to be –
So tender you do becalm my wearied soul.

My heart did pine in want of you,
And in faith and hope I did wait for you.
My eyes looked but it was my heart that saw
You alone, as only you could ever be.

My heart is always on that fire of want
Trying to plunge out of its bony cage.
Sweet dreams which like nightmares had come to be,
Invaded my tormented soul at will.

Your demeanor like a moon that fails to wane
Pose unchecked against this cloudless void.
Your hidden blush the color of my bleeding heart
Tells of how you seem to feel of me.

Your eyes as cloudy as the cloudless skies,
Often as cuprous as the diving sun,
Did announce the arrival of that enigmatic love
That's understood and yet is never unraveled.

PART 2

I see my heart like a bird aimlessly fly
As if on the wings of the fleetly wind.
Where it goes it does not really know
As it uncontrollably soars above –
Aimlessly to that land of nowhere-
That melting pot of all emotions
Where love is the final distillate
Of all those emotions put together.

Love is an everlasting debacle
Of which I believe am still a novice.
You've stirred up some soothing feelings in me,
You've stirred up all those latent feelings
And your love has reared its head in me
And I feel it better and tastier than
A flagon of that ambrosia of the gods.

Please do not say no to me
And become a fulfillment of all my desires
For you have ravished my panting soul.

When last I checked my troubled heart
It only beat just because of you.
It is on fire with your ravishing love-
Love that I value more than life itself.
My waning heart in throbs do ache
To my feelings put in full confusion.
My thoughts have numb become
To all else but you and you alone -
Yet I toil through my sleepless nights alone.

Come to me O my love!!
Please come to me!
For to calm my wearied soul.

Yours,
TJ.

That did the trick!

Cynthia read through and absorbed all those sweet words in the card after Funke had delivered it to her. They immediately took control of her emotions. She read through the card several times over having never in her wildest imaginations believed that someone would write such sweet poems to her. Thomas was indeed her man though she had known that all along. He was her one and only hero.

That night, she slept with the card under her pillow. She probably believed that it might generate some sweet dreams for her, which of course she had. She was in love.

Thomas, on his part tried to avoid her as much as possible after having sent that card. He was not too sure that sending that card was the right thing to do. He was not even sure of what effect it was going to have on her. Supposing it was going to extract the same reaction as that stupid blunder about kissing her, though he did not know why she felt that way. To him, a kiss was a kiss and it was no big deal, just that old harmless kiss. Well with the outbreak of the Ebola virus infection it could no longer be considered as harmless.

The possible outbreak of this epidemic was now the talk of the town. It was on every lip, and the country had just declared a state of emergency just for it. That was surprising though, since it was not even beyond traces in number and the few cases so far involved those who handled the only one transit case that had chanced into the country. What a nasty virus! Delicate as it might be regarding survival outside the body, it makes up for this with its unprecedented ease of transmission, virulence and fatality. Anyway, it is said that a stitch in time saves nine. That seemed to be the position of the government when it came to controlling that epidemic.

No matter what was going to be her reaction, whether good or bad, he was not ready for that and he was not comfortable enough to try and find out for the heart, mind and love have collectively and independently been there as uncharted territories. Anything was possible. No one can guess what would be the reaction or what it was going to do.

Now that the card had been delivered and he was on edge, he wished that he did not send it to her. He would have loved to retrieve it, but there was no way that it could be possible. The egg was already scrambled and there was no way to unscramble it. She had gotten hold of the card and she had already read it. He just had to live with that fact as a mixture of anxiety, uncertainty and nervousness had taken hold of the better part of him.

Thomas did eventually find out the result of his card, but it was in a very odd but welcome way and situation. It was when their school played a football match against their archrival Santa Monica Secondary School. It was a rivalry that started when the two schools were built. Each school would prefer to loose all their matches for the season as long as they were able to beat the other. Santa Monica actually had to make this policy official. Beating the Pentecostals was always their greatest achievement for any given season. When this was put to the ballot, the students voted overwhelmingly to loose the trophy as long as they were able to beat their archrival.

Thomas was not one of the best footballers in their school. In fact he was not a good footballer at all. As luck would have it, they did not have natural left players and he was one of the few. They therefore always put him in the reserve bench just in case some one is injured so that they could use him just to make up the number of players required in the field. For this match, he was there to fill in for any of the left players.

The match did go on as anticipated and it was extremely physical. It was only two minutes to the end of the match that their left halfback was tackled down. He broke his ankle and that was it for him. The game was scoreless so far and the Pentecostals only prayed that it should remain so for the remaining six minutes – two minutes to the end of the match and the four minutes injury time.

Thomas was brought in, and for the next four and a half minutes the ball never went to his side not to talk of his touching it. It was at this moment that there was a goal – mouth tussle at their goalmouth. The Santa captain and center forward managed to beat their goalkeeper just two feet to the goal line. Just as he was about to tap it in, a vicious sliding tackle came out of nowhere. Their right full back was inside the goalmouth and what he did was to deliver a vicious but safe tackle that sent the ball flying out of their danger zone towards the center.

The Santas were already jubilating for the goal before agony came over them. The Pentecostals were the ones that were now jubilating. Inadvertently and obviously mistakenly, the ball made it straight to where Thomas was loitering around the vicinity of the centerline.

He trapped the ball, but there was no one to pass it to. Everyone had gone to attend to that goalmouth tussle except for him, the opposing right full back and the opposing goalkeeper. Since there was no one to pass the ball to, he headed for their opponents goalmouth. He somehow managed to sell a dummy and dribble past that right full back. How he did that, he was not very sure of, but there he was heading for that goalmouth. In fact, he did not even realize that he had dribbled past someone. He learnt of that from the stories that were told later.

Thomas finally kicked the ball wildly towards the right side of the goalmouth from way out. He was afraid that some players were about to catch up with him, though there were none after him and that was why he had to kick the ball. It was an involuntary action. Just like a miracle, which, most were sure that it was, the goalkeeper dived to the other side. Even more miraculously still, the ball slid quietly into the net. The gods of football had done their job!

That was the winning and only goal of the match. The referee already had his whistle in his mouth to blow for the end of the game and so he blew for both at once – the goal and the end that is.

Both players and spectators stormed the pith in uncontrollable frenzy. They carried Thomas shoulder high dancing round the field as their hero. They danced all around the arena till they got tired and finally set him down at the far end of the arena. They called him the giant killer; for that was the first time that they were able to beat the Santas in near to fifteen years.

Lo and behold they had set him down right in front of Cynthia. Quite uncharacteristically and unexpectedly born out of the euphoria and excitement of this memorable game, she simply clasped her arms round his neck and planted one heck of a kiss right on his lips. It was surely the product of that uncontrollable frenzy that followed that occasion. It was much later that Thomas confessed that he nearly fainted from that unexpected kiss.

Cynthia could not tell what came over her and so she simply turned tails and beat it to her hostel. She had done the unthinkable. She had sinned unknowingly and she just could not figure out how or why it happened. Before this incident she could never have imagined herself kissing a boy not to talk of her initiating it. She was worried and this lasted for a few days. During this period she avoided everybody especially Thomas.

She had set her ears to the ground to find out any gossips about that incident. She did not hear anything, just that many of the girls were jealous of her.

Most of the boys envied Thomas. It was not just for becoming the school's hero, but also in connection with that girl who was very beautiful and was the most reserved girl in the school. Had the school authorities noticed that kiss, they would have both been expelled from the school. Not minding his academic shortcomings, Thomas had become the most song hero in the school. He however tried to lie low. He was not sure of why he wanted to lie low, but it could have been a change of character setting in and Cynthia must have influenced it. To him, that kiss was more important than the goal that he had scored.

It was now time for sleepless nights. He both dreamt and daydreamed at night, always seeing himself with Cynthia. At times he would be of the impression that his dreams had fused with his fancies to result in visions. It was all wishful thinking.

In the case of Cynthia, she found solace in hanging about most of the time with her closest friend Funke. Funke was indeed a very trusted friend. She had advised her to be careful since she had become the most celebrated girl in the school. Many, out of jealousy, might try to plot against her, if not through physical harm then through blackmail. Any of the girls could do anything to switch places with her. She was not that type and so she did not see what made that a big deal.

It took quite some time before Cynthia and Thomas came across each other again. Though she still kept him within eyesight, she did not want any encounter with him yet.

The school used boreholes for its water supply, but recently they started scooping petroleum oil from the top of the water. It was for this reason that the school ordered the students to start using water from a stream that was not far behind the school compound. It was on their way to the stream that they met each other. Cynthia was with Funke, while Thomas was with his friend Ribadu.

Funke was one of those girls that hovered around the boundary when it came to beauty. She was tall and well proportioned, but not fat as such. As for her face, it was not in the beautiful range though she was not ugly. As a boxer she was also a bit on the muscular side due to extreme workouts and weight lifting.

Her friendship to Cynthia tended to lend credence to the suggestion that people at times make. It was to the effect that if a pretty girl wanted to look even prettier without makeup, all she has to do is to make friends with and go about with an ugly girl. Her friend's ugliness will tend to accentuate her beauty. Cynthia was however not in that group that will like to be noticed.

One might also be tempted to think that it was for the same reason that Thomas made friends with Ribadu. In his own case it might be more plausible since he was a playboy of sorts and would always want to be noticed. In fact in Ribadu's case, even an ugly boy going about with this anemic and rickety looking thing will instantly change his ugliness to handsomeness. He always looked as if he was about to snap into two. In fact he always looked like one who just came out of a famine stricken area.

That was however his stature. Some of the students even went as far as to claiming that he was suffering from an infestation of rare two-headed intestinal worms. Contrary to all these, his father was actually a shipping magnet that owned a fleet of ten oil supertankers and one luxury cruise ship. He also owned a cement-manufacturing factory in the country.

Thomas, as soon as he saw them in front, arranged with Ribadu to catch up with them and then take Funke aside so that he could talk to Cynthia. After some greetings and the exchange of pleasantries from the now shy Cynthia, Thomas got her to allow him carry her bucket along with his own. This was a gentlemanly act and he was one at times.

On noticing that, Ribadu did the same for Funke. It was Thomas that finally broke the relevant ice:

"Thanks Cynthia."

"For what?" She had asked.

"For that kiss."

Once more she came up with one of those her invisible blushes that conditions of nature would not allow one to see.

"Oh, that?"

"Yes that. And thanks again. I really appreciated it. I've had sleepless nights since then, if you know what I mean."

"It actually came at the spur of the moment and I still can't quite believe that it was me that did that."

"Now that it is obvious that you can't undo that, can I be given the opportunity for a return kiss?"

"No!!"

"Why?"

"You should know better. It is not morally sound to do that."

"But it might look as if you were taking advantage of me if I don't return it."

"In what way?"

"By kissing me voluntarily and not allowing me to do the same. You have done your wish and I am not allowed to do mine."

"Ha-ha-ha. Whom are you trying to trap? Not me for sure."

"Which trap?"

"I am not sure that I will like to follow you into that your sinful world."

"But it's not a sin."

"Said who?"

"Have you forgotten that it's just like any other handshake in the Western world?"

"That is because they want it to be that way most of the time. For us here, and for you in particular, it is not the same."

"Okay then. Let me kiss you in place of a handshake."

"To be candid, there is really nothing wrong with the act, it is what one has in mind while doing it that decides on whether it is going to be a sin."

"In that case I will try to leave my mind blank while kissing you."

"It seems as if you don't plan to give up."

"Well, if I give up on what I want and on what has become a part of me and my fantasies, then I must be crazy."

It was at that stage that she remembered what could make them leave that topic alone. Maybe it will work, maybe not. It would be worth trying anyway.

"By the way, thanks for that valentine card. I am sorry it is now a belated thanks."

"It's my pleasure. Did you like it?"

"Do you want to hear the truth?"

"Yes. The truth, the whole truth and nothing but the truth."

She then lowered her face and turned sideways as if she was afraid that he might be able to read her mind.

"I slept with it under my pillow for three days. It is now in a safe corner inside my box. I even brought it out this morning for another look. Thanks again for that."

"You are welcome."

"Maybe next year it will be my turn to send one to you."

"I can't wait for that."

"Me too. It's going to be like an eternity to me."

They were now almost by the stream when Thomas made his move. He drew her to one side and replanted that one heck of a kiss on her lips. He was no longer in control of his actions and he could not help it. He was ready to damn the consequences, but what happened next more than surprised him as much as it excited him. She had immediately thrown her arms around his neck in total surrender before suddenly turning away. It was a fairly short one, but she had accepted it and that was more than enough for him.

At the stream, he filled both buckets and carried them both back to just outside the school gate. Ribadu and Funke had been watching and they had imitated those two right from the kisses to carrying the buckets. The only thing was that their kiss lasted much longer.

Size wise, Funke was much bigger than petite Ribadu and she looked like one who could beat up any man that fooled around. Ribadu did not mind that because his moving with her was going to make him one of the boys to be talked about in school. Funke, on her path was going to brag for the other girls, because she had finally got her self a man. Ribadu would do for now, after all it is claimed that half bread is better than none.

Most of the students in the school lived in denial of their true feelings. Most of the girls will give anything to exchange places with Funke for that tender looking Ribadu. In fact he looked rather anemic, but all the same, and once again, half bread was always better than none at all. Any of those girls in the school could always beat him to submission, not to talk of Funke. She was the schools female heavy weight-boxing champion.

Ribadu was well aware of his shortcomings and he often used these to make fun of himself. He once told the other boys of how he used to dream of himself as a married man. He claimed the dream had repeated itself so many times that he believed it was an omen. According to him, he often dreamt of being married to a boxer. His wife was bigger and stronger than he was. He always picked trouble with her just to ascertain his position as the head of the household.

When she finally got fed up with him, she sued him for divorce on the grounds of physical abuse. The judge summoned both of them to court for the case. Just a look at his pitiable anemic condition was enough for him to make up his mind. Apart from that, he had turned up with a black eye. After all deliberations, the judge granted the divorce with no strings attached. He made it clear that this young man had used his hard earned money to buy trouble for himself in the guise of a wife. It would be unfair to ask him to pay alimony or any other thing.

He claimed that he had paid enough both monetarily and physically all through the marriage. He was therefore only trying to free the poor man from the clutches of constant battering from his own wife. He even pointed out that the man was surely insane since no man in his right minds would do what he had done. He still did not see how a sane man could willingly, intentionally and eagerly pay for life-long problems in the name of dowry.

He was therefore freed from his wife with no conditionality or compensations due to either of them. He pointed out, as he told them the story, that he did not have Funke in mind as his wife in the dream.

Blackmail could come from anywhere, and it could come for all sorts of reasons. Jealousy had reared its ugly head at the Pentecostal school. Many boys were now jealous of Thomas just for being the one associated with Cynthia, who was indisputably the prettiest girl in the entire school. The only way they could figure out to put a strain in that relationship and split them was through blackmail. Each and every one of the boys would like to have them split up, but it was only Sunnyboy that was man enough to try and see his wishes go through. His actual name was Sunday Cunnicula, and he was indeed the most cunning boy in the school.

What Sunnyboy did was to theoretically link him up with one particular girl named Nido, though more popularly as Similaac. This was the name that the boys assigned to her because of her outrageously large breasts. They were claimed to be the size of oversized hybrid watermelons and many of these boys believed that she must be a very strong girl. Their reason was that they figured that anyone who could comfortably carryon with those loads must be both tough and abnormally strong.

It was claimed, though this was never substantiated, that she once expressed out over two gallons of mothers milk from them daily for seven days. The milk was freeze -dried and sealed up in metal cans as dry instant baby milk. It was a fake baby milk company that processed them and also marketed them as Similaac.

Similaac's real name was Humongez Epistopolus. Her father was probably Greek and her mother from one of the Latin American countries. There was really nothing about her for one to write home about. The boys in general had that tendency to keep away from her.

Sunnyboy had got the rumor going that during the last vacation, Humongez was sighted in an abortion clinic and that not long after that she headed for the Similaac manufacturer to make a little money to offset what she spent in the clinic. It was claimed that she had gone through a couple of boys, especially those that were after cheap scores, and so was not sure of which particular boy was responsible for her pregnancy. Her father had therefore conducted a DNA paternity test and it turned out that Thomas was the father of the fetus.

A fake copy of this test result had somehow managed to find its way into the school and was circulating secretly amongst the boys. This rumor spread like wild fire and in no time Cynthia came to hear about it. She sort of confirmed this rumor when she tried to find out the truth from three other girls. Each of them was unhappy with Thomas for descending so low. She therefore managed to call Thomas aside for a one-on-one discussion of the issue:

"Thomas, there is a rumor circulating in the school that you put Humongez into family way." Cynthia told him.

"Me?"

"Yes. According to them, you were responsible for that."

"How did you know that she was pregnant?"

"The nurse who works at the doctor's office where she went for the abortion happened to be a sister to Michael.

I hope you know Michael. Michael Gossiinpa, and he was the person who leaked the news to the rest of the students."

"I am learning about that pregnancy for the first time now."

"It seems that you are trying to be very cagey with your answers and also reluctant about talking of it. It seems you find it embarrassing."

"Yes, I find it embarrassing to discuss such topics."

"Don't tell me that you feel that way because you fear that it might be true." He chuckled before answering her:

"Cynthia, are you telling me that even if the devil appears to you and tells you that I had committed adultery you will believe him?"

"But this story is not from the devil."

"And why don't you think twice before you make up your mind?"

"In what way?"

"Do you really believe that even at gunpoint I will agree to have anything to do with that girl?"

"I was certain that you had been framed, it's just that I wanted you to take action. When I heard it, I told myself that you would have dismissed the rumor as lacking merit. You would have asked how possible it could be for one to have a glass of champagne in front of him and yet he would ask for a glass of water used to wash a glass of wine. That's the comparison between me and her as far as I am concerned."

"I guess you've made your point."

"Trust me."

"So why on earth did you really ask?"

"Just for the fun of it too."

Thomas chuckled once more before saying with determination:

"Just give me two days and I will give you a result. I will find out whoever it is that had framed me up."

"Please take care."

"Trust me." I will be very careful with the investigation.

Thomas went into action right away and within a few hours he had traced the origin of the rumor to Sunnyboy. It was time to retaliate.

He was resolved on paying him back in kind, but his own had to be more damaging. There was a pregnant mad woman that begs at the road junction to the school and he was going to link her up with Sunnyboy. He let his own rumor take flight right away. In the rumor, it was claimed that the mad woman used to call Sunnyboy "my husband" whenever he passed by. The mad woman fell sick and was taken to the hospital where they found out that she had AIDS. The AIDS clinic was therefore forced to find out who was responsible for her pregnancy. That was a simple way of keeping AIDS in check.

According to the rumor, the woman insisted that Sunnyboy was her only lover and husband and so a DNA test was conducted. He was the father and so they had to test him for AIDS. He was still awaiting the result. He made sure that the rumor should always be linked up to him.

It was not long before this juicy news item went round the entire school and Sunnyboy was hurt and ashamed. He had no time to waste and so he called on Thomas for a truce. Thomas asked him to go and apologize to both Similaac and Cynthia, and go right ahead to tell the other students that it was a false rumor that he concocted out of jealousy. He was quick to do that, and then Thomas told the school that he invented the story about Sunnyboy in retaliation for his own false rumors.

Cynthia's heart had now been put at full rest. It was only after this that she decided that what she learnt from the whole episode was that detractors could always strike in any manner, from anywhere and at any time. When Thomas came over to her, it was only to make sure that Sunnyboy had fully apologized. She there and then vowed never to suspect him again no matter the odds. She will always take his words as true.

As for Cynthia and Thomas, this their relationship continued that way till they went into their senior class in the school.

THE PUBLIC HOLIDAYS

It had suddenly occurred to these two people that they were now adults, Cynthia and Thomas that is. Each of them was now eighteen years old and it was time for them to start taking decisions on their own. Their relationship had been purely platonic in line with all Christian expectations and principles. Thomas had also significantly reduced the rate at which he talked to the other girls. He dearly loved Cynthia and he did everything possible to make sure that she would never be in the know as to any other thing he did.

They were now in their final year in school and a four-day mid-term break was coming up. They conferred and decided to spend it at Onono Island. This was a very small island that was formed out of sand and silt in the middle of one of their majestic rivers. It was a flat expanse that was high above the water level under full exposure to the tropical sun. Very soft white sand ringed the island, which had a clump of shrubs in the middle.

Between this clump of shrubs and the sand was a fairly small house. This house did not look impressive from the outside, but it was lavishly furnished with no consideration given to money. They were already in a speedboat headed for the island before Cynthia informed Thomas that the island belonged to her father. It was the first time of her telling him anything about her father for she had always been overtly protective as to his identity.

Christian Rodriguez, her father, finished from high school essentially as a dropout. Not minding the fact that he had no relevant qualification to get him into the university, his father managed to get him into one. There he started studying economics. This was possible because his father was the chairman of the board of regents for the school. It was the most exclusive university in Spain then. It was the Agenda University, and money had spoken. Christian was however too business minded to concentrate on his academic works and so he ended up as an average "E" student. He had always remained in that range, and he was satisfied with it anyway.

He however managed to amass quite some wealth. Within that first year in school, he had made almost ten million dollars from various business transactions, which were between him and the other students. The undergraduates were his clienteles.

By the time his father found out what was going on, it was already too late for him to continue in the school. His father was a very practical man. Rather than get annoyed with him, he introduced him to one of his friends, an Arab oil sheik. He quickly relocated to the sheik's emirate and within a year he had made them proud of him.

The highest that the emirate had ever made from oil in a year was about one billion dollars, within the last ten years. That was when there was civil war in one of the oil producing emirates and the Organization of Petroleum Exporting Countries – OPEC – decided to raise oil prices. It had claimed that the rise was simply in line with the laws of supply and demand. Incidentally Armageddon, which was the name of the emirate that Rodriguez had relocated to, had a population of less than one million.

For that first year when the Emir had named him the grand overseer of their oil sector, they made thirteen billion dollars. The Emir was so impressed by this performance that he let Rodriguez have a bonus of one billion dollars for that his first year there. That was the beginning of his wealth. He used to be rich as a student, but he was now wealthy. Rodriguez quickly started his own private oil companies in other oil-rich countries. Within a year he had diversified into other areas.

With time, he got married to Rose Cynthia Barnacles. About a year later they had Cynthia junior, and barely four years after that, Cynthia senior died in a private plane accident. Rodriguez vowed never to remarry.

She then told him of how she lived at home. She owned three chauffeured cars. Her father bought that island as a resort where he used to go and hide whenever it was time for rest from his near permanent flying around the world.

Thomas was overwhelmed and flabbergasted by these revelations. He knew that Cynthia was rich, but not to that extent. They managed to spend the entire vacation there on the island studying and perusing the scriptures, which was the only area that he was good at. He was well at home with anything from the bible. Thomas would not normally be eager to study the scriptures, but the power of love had started to change and shape his outlook. Whatever she wanted was what he liked. He will never do anything that could make her uncomfortable, not to talk of unhappy.

On the third day, they decided to leave the island for the first time. One of her cars was there to take them out to an amusement park and from there to a film theatre. Towards the end of the day, they returned to the island and lay on the beach to watch the sun set in the west. This had become their daily ritual, including watching it rise in the east every morning.

On this particular day, the sky was very clear and the sun had hardly dipped into that western horizon before the stars began to twinkle their ways out. They tended to twinkle shyly, probably because they were afraid of the sun that was still there. Everywhere was the color of bronze except for the east that presented predominantly with the towering skyscrapers of the city. It had always been a mesmerizing spectacle to behold the day die.

That night, after a sumptuous meal from their cook, they decided to retire to their respective rooms early in preparation for going back to the school the following day. Before going in however they had decided to curl up on the sofa to let the meal digest a little bit. During this period they watched an African Magic Chanel film. The title was: "*Ije mu na love*' – The Journey between me and love. It was predominantly in Ibo language with English sub-titles. What an appropriate title for these two.

In a nutshell, it was the story about a lady who had sought for love in all possible places but never found it. She however, by an act of fate, eventually found her prince charming from the most unexpected of all places. This happened after she had actually given up. She was going to die as a rich single lady. She lived alone in a big house, a house that could very easily be seen as too big for her. To keep fit she had decided to have no house helps as she did everything by herself.

There was this male beggar that always sat under a tree, a little bit beyond her house. She always dropped some loose change into his pan for him. His beards were so bushy that they essentially hid his face. Whenever she dropped anything for him, he would thank her by saying: "Thank you very much and may the Lord grant you your wishes."

On this fateful morning, it was a public holiday, as she was driving out for some groceries, she could not tell what came over her and she compassionately dropped ten one thousand naira notes into his pan. As he noticed how much it was, he ran after her to explain that she must have made a mistake. She told him that it was not a mistake and refused to take the money back as he tried to hand it back to her. According to her, she gave the money just as the spirit moved her. He thanked her again and danced back to his stand.

While driving to the store, she kept thinking. Why was that beggar so honest? Any other person would have taken the money and check out from there for fear of her coming back to look for it. Apart from that, why did he have such a refined accent? He was surely honest to a fault. She finally made up her mind on how to help that beggar. She was going to take her chances and employ him. She planned to let him take care of the house and compound once a week for a fair stipend.

After she got home from her shopping, she went out on foot and asked the beggar to come and help her carry her purchases into her house because they were many and a few were too heavy for her to carry. While he was helping her with offloading her purchases, she told him about her plan to employ him. The man accepted immediately and looked rather very excited.

Just out of curiosity, she asked him about his past. She said that as an employer it was only right to find that out. He was to take it as an interview that she should have conducted before hiring him. What she found out surprised her.

Samuel, as he called himself, was a graduate with a master's degree in international relations. He had no siblings and both his parents died in a motor accident on their way from his graduation ceremony. Due to the economic situation in the country, he was a job seeker for four years but found no employment. It was during this period that he found out that panhandling was a fairly lucrative venture.

He made close to fifty thousand naira monthly from this, and with the money he rented a room where he kept his few belongings. That was where he slept every night. She was touched.

She had bought a few things for him and she asked him when he would like to resume. The answer was right away. She then convinced him to use one of her bathrooms and wash up and change into the new clothing she had bought for him. She also had shaving blades.

What she saw when he eventually came out from the bathroom took her aback. She was more than pleasantly surprised. He was definitely much younger than he used to look with those beards and he had a sort of deliciously handsome face.

As it is at times put, with time, one thing led to another and so within three months the wedding bell had tolled between them. Just as such stories also went, they lived happily as husband and wife ever after.

Cynthia loved that story line, though she felt that in her own case, she never went for any prince charming before getting one. Thomas was her man and he was her life. She was now beginning to fantasize on when they were going to get married too.

"If beating about the bush is my lot then let it be history for I am going to hit the nail on the head as it were." That was Thomas talking to Cynthia. He was under the influence of that film.

"In what way?"

"Just looking for a way to assure you once more that I love you."

"Me too."

"I am also ready to do anything for you. Even if you do not believe me, I am ready to lay down my life for you."

"Please don't."

"Why?"

"Should that ever happen, I am likely going to join you right away."

"I believe you, and I will never leave you."

"What can I do without you?"

"Anything you wish to do."

"Shut up. At least you know what I mean."

"Honestly speaking, I don't."

"It seems that I think of you so much that it is now the thought of you that keeps me going."

"How sweet of you," he retorted as she smiled, "you seem to have just echoed back my thoughts for it is the same with me."

"Wow, you seem to have a way of putting things and that makes me feel that you are the best thing that has happened to me ever."

"To me, you are the best thing that has ever come my way."

"I love you Cynthia."

"I love you too." She then blew a kiss across to him.

"I believe that it is time for us to do something about this my feeling."

"Something like what?"

"How can I know?"

"If you don't know, is there any reason why I should?"

"Supposing we match to the chapel right away and there ask the pastor to unite us in holy matrimony."

"Ha-ha-ha."

"And what's so funny about that?"

"Don't you think that you are simply jumping the gun?"

"In what way?"

"But the only responsible thing to do is to start by telling our parents about our intentions."

"You got me there."

"Anyway one of these days it might come down to that, but first things first."

"Like what?"

"Our education."

"You know the best thing for us."

The following day they took off and went back to the school.

The company of the other had delighted each of them. Right now, they could not exist for more than twenty-four hours without seeing each other. They were totally committed and in love with each other.

Barely two weeks after this mid term break; they had another two days to kill. This time around, it was a two-day Muslim holidays. Cynthia had suggested that they go on a sight seeing adventure of the countryside and he had accepted. Cynthia therefore called one of her chauffeurs to come and pick them up from the school for a drive around. This one came in a red colored Rolls Royce. Thomas could not contain himself when the car came around. It was going to be his first ride in that car. He had heard of it but had never really seen one, not to talk of riding about in it.

The driver had waited for them just outside the school gate. As the chauffeur jumped out to open the doors for them, he slipped, fell down and got his uniform soiled. That was enough to attract the attention of many students, and they were all eyes when they saw the car. Her instruction to the driver was that they should simply drive around through their usual route and soak in the countryside.

They did not drive through any of the major roads; instead they took mainly the unpaved country lanes. This gave them the opportunity to savor the pristine countryside. By one of the many types of seashore there, they stopped and waded through the ebbing brackish waters. It was time for a little bit of nature study. The most striking thing here were tree pneumatophores that jutted out through the low water. These were breathing roots for the trees. They would usually be submerged at high tide.

Crabs of various sizes were abundant there together with what looked like millions of fish fries. They were safe there, away from the bigger fish that will find the water there too shallow. These bigger ones would normally eat them. The best lesson that Cynthia derived from what was going on there was that nature always had a way of taking care of its own.

What impressed Thomas most was the way that the fish fries dashed off in various choreographed formations at the slightest disturbance. They finally tried a little bit of angling. The chauffeur had come along with some rods, lines and bait. Cynthia managed to catch a small tilapia fish as well as a table-sized catfish. As for Thomas, his luck shined when he managed to reel in an old abandoned shoe. They all found it funny because he looked very excited as he pulled it in before changing to surprised disappointment on seeing what it was. Most of the big fish, as he was to learn later, were either hiding amongst roots and caves or out into the deeper waters.

At another spot, they stopped to watch an eagles nest from binoculars. The last time that Cynthia was there a pair were trying to build a nest. It had long been completed and there was a young nearly fully-grown eagle in it. As they watched, one of the parents, ostensibly the female, circled in and landed with a fairly sized fish on its talons. It tore it up and swallowed the bigger chunks while giving the smaller chunks to the young one. Just before they finished, another adult came in. It was carrying a very big rabbit on its talons. They believed it was the male. It dropped the rabbit for the other two and perched aside. There was a lot of noise before they settled down to dine on it. Thomas believed that they were only congratulating the male for the big catch.

Cynthia finally explained to Thomas that the two adults were mates and that they usually mated for life. Thomas remained pensive as she explained this. His thoughts were on the line that they too were probably on their way to becoming mates for life too. Cynthia probably had the same thoughts too, because when their eyes met, each seemed to be confused, shy and anxious all at once. Each of them was probably wishing that the other could voice out those feelings but that never happened. Instead of that, they both got up and hurried back to the car without looking at each other. The journey had to continue.

They finally got to Cynthia's most favorite spot. It was a flat rolling expanse that was lushly green with flower heads all over. The flowers came in all imaginable hues, shapes and patterns. Some were not odoriferous at all while others were very fragrant. They both quickly ran through the wild flowers sniffing at them. Bees and butterflies seemed to be having a field day there too. A few birds were around to pick up some insects.

It was while they were at this that Thomas somehow managed to pluck a white flower. He stuck it into Cynthia's hair. This immediately extracted one of those her invisible blushes, together with other telltale facial expressions that she would have loved to keep to herself. She felt both shy and happy at the same time. Thomas was battling with his panting breath as well as his throbbing heart in an attempt to figure out what to say. He eventually managed to make it:

"It is lovely here and you are very lovely."

"I've been waiting for you to say something."

"I will always miss this place."

"That's why I always come this way. I can never have enough of it."

"I will definitely miss you when schooling is over"

There was a short lull in the diatribe, which lasted as if it was eternity before she resumed:

"Thanks for the flower."

"I actually have not yet figured out why or how I managed to do that."

"I guess I know why."

"Please help me out."

"Do you really love me?"

"Should I say yes, that would be an understatement."

"That means that you love me then?"

"Without being told."

"I am aware of that. I just wanted to hear you say it again and I love you too. I know that the flower was presented to me as a way of your saying that. I am impressed by your choice of color too. The white was to hint on the fact that it was pure love. Thanks again."

"You are welcome."

He accepted that analysis though he actually had nothing like that in mind when it happened. It just happened to be the first flower that his hand reached when he thought of giving her one. It is obvious that girls seem to have that ability to think more deeply when it came to the issues of the heart than the boys. Knowing Thomas, at least the Thomas that he used to be, it could have as well been a simple prank. Anyway who are we to delve into LOVE'S UNCHARTED TERRITORIES?

Further down, they chanced on a small brook. It was indeed a very small one. It sallied forth from a small clump of reeds. The water was very clear as it lazily wound its way in-between the tender stems of many flowers. In fact, it barely flowed. The water was so clear that its white sandy bed looked as if there was no water at all flowing over it. He looked and searched for, but did not see even a single fish in the water. Maybe it was one of those fair weather brooks, though the path it followed did not lend to that idea. He bent down and scooped a little of the water into the cup of his hand. He tasted it and it was almost cold as well as blandly delicious. It was the best pure water that he had ever tasted.

Cynthia watched with curiosity as he did that. He bent down for another scoop. This time around he offered it to Cynthia. She took a sip off the cup of his hand. She nodded, then smiled before saying:

"I never knew that water could taste so delicious."

"That was why I wanted you to have a sip. I didn't believe it either."

"Maybe it tasted that way to me because it came from you."

"No way."

"Nothing could be so delicious except probably you."

"But you are yet to taste me."

Thomas finally believed that he had just got a lead to build on. He was going to push it and see how far he could go, but she was much faster than he was. She had already realized that she should not have put it that way. She therefore replied:

"It's all in the imagination, but anyway if we don't hurry up to get back to school then we might get locked out."

She did not wait for any reaction or answer before turning and running back to the car. He had no choice but to run after her disappointed. To him, it did not seem to be getting late and he believed that she was just aiming for an escape route. He was wrong.

Their next stop was her favorite outpost eatery – "Waziri's Kitchen of a Thousand Delights." They were all already hungry or rather famished. They both went in and sat at one corner while the chauffeur who entered later chose the opposite corner. There were no other customers there. They had hardly touched the call bell on their table when a fairly voluminous lady came in from the kitchen door. She came to their table and handed over the menu list to them while saying:

"Please make your choices and Waziri's wife will make your wishes come true in a jiffy."

They took a look at the list together and Cynthia asked Thomas:

"What would you have Thomas?"

"After you." He replied.

"No. As my guest here it is your choice that matters."

"But I am not exactly your guest since we are, as it were, one."

"I insist."

"Okay then, what of ladies first?"

"And what of men as the heads of the families?"

"But I am not yet a man, going by my age."

"Okay my lawyer, I will choose for both of us."

"Whatever you choose will be the best for me."

She acknowledged that with a smile before announcing her choice. All one had to do here was to pick up the ingredients and that lady will transform them into a delicious concoction. Her choices were:

Partridge – Lamb soup as appetizer, to be supported with chicken dumpling and extra dry grape juice.

For the main course she chose: Spicy tender chicken thighs, Rice pilaf with tender green Lima beans, seasoned smoked Salmon with a side dish of Bitter leaf soup. It was this last bit that excited Thomas most. It was the most popular soup in that area of the country, and he got used to it through his father. It was his father's usual Sunday afternoon treat. He claimed that it had an uncanny way of calming him down after all that marathon and strenuous sermon. There is really nothing about that soup except to point out that it often had that elusive taste that tends to remind one of a hint of the heavens, that is if one knows what the heavens taste like.

For dessert she had chosen hot ash-softened black African pears together with garden egg leaf salad and yoghurt in place of salad cream. This dessert often has that tendency to bring back to the palate an after taste of all the other things already eaten, both individually and collectively.

Within the hour, they were each so stuffed up that they found it hard to move from their seats, the chauffeur included. They only managed to get back to school just before the gates were locked. Thomas thanked her for making it a very memorable day for him, while she thanked him for making her day worth it. They finally parted for their respective hostels.

As Thomas was to confess much later, he had spent that night very much awake while trying to count the ceiling tiles in the dark. He had claimed that he just could not get the thoughts of Cynthia off his mind, not even for a single moment. Remembering her had simply stolen sleep from his eyes. He had tossed around all through the night as was evidenced by his bedspreads. They were rumpled and lay all over the floor by his bedside in the morning.

Incidentally Cynthia had spent her night in a similar manner for they were both deeply in love with each other.

BITTER ENCOUNTERS

It was not long after the Muslim holidays before the two lovers finished from their secondary school. They worked briefly in different offices before setting off for the university.

Cynthia was so brilliant and academically sound that she was able to set a few records in school. First of all, she was the only student in school to ever pass the Latin class with a score of one hundred percent. Their Latin teacher used to reserve a mark of minus ten percent for each of the students before marking the papers. He termed that "The Universal Imperfection Factor." No man is ever perfect.

Latin was the most dreaded subject in the school, and its teacher was even more dreaded as a human being. He was a patented miser when it came to marks in tests and examinations. In one test, Cynthia actually corrected him on the question before answering it. The second highest scorer got forty percent while Cynthia corrected it and scored one hundred percent. Incidentally, the teacher had given Cynthia ten percent for her correction and that offset the universal imperfection factor.

At the final external school certificate examination, Cynthia did not disappoint anyone. Everyone was to choose a minimum of eight out of the fifteen available subjects that year. The second best result was from a boy who scored "A" in six out of the eight subjects that he took and "B" in each of the remaining two. Cynthia took all fifteen subjects and scored "A" in all fifteen.

Every university wanted Cynthia. This was because of her scores in the common admission tests, and they included the schools she applied to and those she did not apply to as well as the ones she had never heard of. She had a perfect score and was fifteen points clear of the second best entrant out of over a million candidates.

She eventually had to opt for the most prestigious of all the schools. This was the All Saints University. It was an exclusive school with a total campus population of only one thousand students that were tutored by well over four hundred lecturers. She was admitted to study medicine and every undergraduate there was on full scholarship.

Thomas could not secure any university admission because he could not make any of the cut off points. He could not even make that range that would qualify some to retake the examinations at no extra cost. Since the university had eluded him, he headed for the state owned school of arts to study for an Ordinary National Diploma in sociology. According to his father, the only thing he seemed good at was to attend all social occasions and that might help a little bit in sociology. Should he do well there, then he would have the option for a direct entry into the university.

Thomas and Cynthia saw each other once in a while. They had taken a vow to remain lovers for life. Cynthia had purchased two smart phones, one for each of them, for use in their communicating with each other. They did so on a daily basis while spending all their vacations together, usually in Cynthia's house. They also visited Thomas's parents on occasions.

It is claimed that he who has dedicated his life to wearing white robes does not go in search of tie-and-dye fabrics. Thomas had dedicated his life to Cynthia and he was in love with her. She was the apple of his eyes, and to him, she was whiter than snow when it came to character and beauty too. In comparison, all the other girls seemed wanting one way or the other and he no longer took interest in looking at them. He had unbelievably moved into a sort of monogamous relationship.

In this school of the arts, he never fraternized with any of the female students. He knew that he loved Cynthia, but he did not realize how deeply he loved her till he was sent suddenly for some rotations at the All Saints University. He was given but for just a few minutes notice to go there and so he decided to surprise her and see how surprised she would be on seeing him suddenly and unexpectedly.

They had been so madly in love with each other that each had assumed that nothing, and nothing whatsoever, could ever separate them. They respected each other's feelings and tolerated each other's shortcomings.

It is claimed that there are always two sides to every coin and that seems to be true with love too. What comes next is a presentation of the other side, the ugly side of love. This helps to point an accusing finger at love and show that when it comes to love and the mind nothing could be expected and that it is indeed an uncharted territory. Love is sweet, but it could also be bitter, it could be tolerating but could be intolerant. In other words, just like the coin it is two sided and at times more so, it could be more than two sided.

Love could be tolerant, but just a small trigger could make it totally intolerant. It is patient, but it could at times be in a hurry to be fulfilled. It is more often forgiving but it could very easily change to vengeance, and this also goes with its being peaceful while at the same time it could lead to anger and mistrust.

Though full of happiness and joy, one single misstep could change it to unhappiness and sadness. Under such circumstances, it could change from being an open relationship to becoming a very secretive one. It saves lives and defends it just as it could as well, in anger, lead to murder.

Love is loyal, but betrayal is the other side that is often seen when there is a misunderstanding. Thomas was certain that Cynthia had betrayed him as seen from what follows and he changed from being very reasonable to being totally unreasonable. No matter from which side, truthfulness is the basis of love, but with even the slightest misdemeanor, untruthfulness and lies surface. Should these not hold, then jealousy sets in and it could change from being long lasting and longsuffering to becoming something temporary.

Finally lovers live as if they breathe conscience, but misadventures could result in actions that are carried out without recourse to conscience.

From all the above, love could therefore be seen as an equivocating phenomenon. It could shift sides in an instance without warning and so is highly unpredictable. Delving into it is therefore like moving into an uncharted territory. The following is an adventure into this uncharted territory.

When Thomas got to the All Saints University, he went straight to Cynthia's room. It was going to be a surprise visit, as he knew that she would be in the room at that time of the day. She was not there. It took a little time for him to remember that she said that she had picked up acting as a way of occupying her mind in other not to think of him all the time. That was how he managed to head for the arts theater.

As he opened the door of the theater, he saw her right away on the stage acting. They were shooting a short historical film. It was about a peasant girl who managed to warm her way into the heart of the Emperor of Kamaluland Empire. She eventually ended up as the Empress while the former Empress was ejected from the palace. Some claimed that the former queen was beheaded for being a witch. Others said that she spent the rest of her life scheming to get back into the palace but was completely unsuccessful to the end.

At the very moment that he stepped in, Cynthia was in the arms of the Emperor as he kissed her. It was a very long passionate-looking kiss. They had to make it look as real as possible. It had taken the film director a very long time to get Cynthia to play that scene.

That was it! How come that this lady who found it hard to give him a befitting kiss, was there at the stage kissing away? Acting or not, it was not acceptable. The man who acted as the Emperor looked much more masculine than himself and that must have been why she was there enjoying herself. This was no acting. It was for real! Love was about to show that its ugly side as he flew off his rockers.

Livid with anger, he stormed out of the theater. He went straight for his room where he lay down. For an entire day he had lost his appetite and did not eat. He had lost the better part of him. His mind actually flirted with the idea of striding to her room and beating her to pulps as well as going over to shoot that Emperor. This second idea did not look too attractive because the man could very easily overpower him, even with one of his hands tied behind him.

Cynthia had seen him as he stormed out of the theater and she ran after him, but he was nowhere to be found. She finally came to the conclusion that it was one of those her fancies. There was no way that he could be there right in the middle of the week.

It was not until the third day before Thomas decided to go and look for her. He did not see why he should remain there languishing in self-inflicted agony while she might be out there enjoying herself. He even thought of committing suicide at one stage. The only thing that kept him from that was what he learnt from his father. Men will not forgive you for doing that and God will punish you for that.

He stood arms akimbo outside her door as he got there, contemplating on what to do with her. After a few minutes, he banged in, but it was only to meet her half-dressed. She was surprised and out of words to see him again and only God knows how he managed not to have given her at least a slap.

"What a surprise!" She shouted as she whirled round and tried to run into his arms, still not fully dressed. He simply sidestepped to avoid her completely. She nearly ran into the door, having been propelled further than anticipated by the momentum of the charge. The surprise further increased as she asked:

"What's wrong my love?"

"Don't pretend that you don't know what is wrong."

"Know what?" She still asked, now getting completely lost. But with his arms once more on akimbo, he commented:

"I did not know that you were like that, you hypocrite."

"What are you talking about, and what has got into you?"

"You pretentious spoilt brat!"

"I am surprised at you. How can you burst into my room only to rain insults at me without explanation?" For once, she was beginning to loose her cool at him, but she made all possible efforts to keep her cool and not shout back.

"You loose girl!" He continued.

"Me?"

"Yes, you."

"Did you smoke or inhale anything?"

"What do you mean by that?"

"Because you are surely not the Thomas that I used to know. By the way, what brought you here?"

"Don't try to change the topic."

"Which topic?"

"Please stop working me up by pretending that you don't know what I am talking about."

"Men are always like that," she thought. They assume a lot by believing that another person will know what they have in mind that they have not said in the first instance.

"But I don't." She finally replied.

With that he stormed out of the room and was gone just as he had come. As he explained much later, he had to get out of there, and very fast too, to avoid committing murder.

Cynthia was preparing to go to the library, but that was all over now. She was too emotionally worked up to be able to do so. The whole issue confused her, and she was getting devastated. She could not imagine where she had gone wrong, but all the same she cried. She sobbed, she wept and she shed tears for what she was not sure of. She only imagined that she was about to loose Thomas and that was enough to make her go crazy if time is not taken. She had become heavy-hearted, sad and above all, very edgy. Was it just an unnecessary panic? Come to think of it, he could have been the one that appeared at the theater and then vanished.

She had lost her appetite and she had stopped eating too. Thomas was just on the verge of breaking her tender heart. She had suddenly become absent minded as tears constantly welled in her eyes. She was getting depressed and could no longer read. She actually tried to go out and look for him, but where could she start to look?

Cynthia had suddenly started talking in her dreams or more likely "day dreams" since she hardly ever sleep at all, not even in the night. Though rather outgoing previously, she had suddenly turned into an introvert. She will not talk to anyone except to lie down on her bed most of the time.

About three days later, as she was going out for her first meal in as many days, she came across Thomas near the café:

"Hello Thomas." She greeted. "I have been looking for you."

"What for?"

"To find out what you were talking about the other day."

"I hope you know that one of my characters is that be it good or bad, I will not mince words to say what I have in mind?"

"I still remember that."

"Okay. Why were you passionately kissing one man the other day in the theater?"

Tears welled up in her eyes as she wanted to reply in-between sobs, but he cut her short as he continued:

"You will normally claim that kissing is immoral and will hardly ever kiss me, but there you were on the stage passionately kissing away." Now she realized that he was the person she saw in the theater.

"But that was just acting Thomas."

"Don't you Thomas me. Why not go all the way with him in the name of acting? Maybe you have been doing so already."

"What has come over you Thomas?"

"It's you."

"Me?"

"Yes you."

"In what way?"

"You have broken my heart by flirting with another man no matter in what way."

"Another man? Where? When?"

"At least with that man with you on the stage."

"Can't you get it into your head that we were just acting? What you saw had nothing to do with love. It is just make believe and it is only you that I love or will ever love."

"I hope you remember that love is jealous."

"I have heard that before."

"That is what is happening to me. As long as you go about kissing other men I do not want to have anything to do with you."

"But you are only making a mountain out of a mole hill or ant hill."

"I am not. Anyway the choice is yours and I cannot force you. Go ahead then and keep messing around with other men. I have had it with you and I should be making my exit."

She then began to cry, but rather than console her, the only thing that came out of his mouth was:

"Please stop shedding those crocodile tears."

She even cried the more. His ranting was surely nothing but the misguided afflatus of a man who had erroneously believed that his woman was cheating on him. He was only licking his imagined wounds that were not there in the first instance.

Thomas had made up his mind there and then to leave Cynthia rather than suffer the more. He might probably end up killing her if he hung around there any longer, though he was probably less broken hearted than she was. It was love that had blinded him and robbed him of his reasoning faculty. His mind had run amuck and it was now dwelling within one of those its uncharted territories – a zone where anything was possible, both good and bad. If not that he had decided to take it like a man, he would have broken down like Cynthia. Unknown to him, she was very innocent and that was what pained her the most.

Though love will normally tolerate a lot, it had shifted to its other side where intolerance and violence dominate.

With time, they both left school and began to work. Thomas had become one of the best workers in his company, but the toll of his loss of Cynthia was about to take place.

Thomas could no longer concentrate or cope with his life and so he ended up seeking solace in the bosom of alcohol and other drugs. He could not get her out of his mind and so he had to shift to these. He was quick to become a drug addict and of course he became very unproductive in his place of work. He had won the best worker of the month for nine consecutive months before this time, but he had suddenly become the worst and was even on the verge of being sacked. He was of course eventually dismissed.

He still contemplated the option of suicide once again, but he was unable to carry it out. First of all, it is very hard for one to kill another human, and it is even more difficult when it comes to one himself. Secondly and more importantly anyway was that part of him that had come off from his fathers preaching about how God would simply not accept it.

As a final solution, he ended up finding himself in the Seminary. He came out of there a priest and he was posted to a remote village to minister to the villagers. He had earlier on in life suffered from Parent Triggered Revolt Control, and now it had resurfaced but in a different form. Having now been influenced by Cynthia Broken Heartedness Syndrome had set in. He ended up no longer able to trust any woman because of this frustration and apparent betrayal from his one and only Cynthia. He was soon going to end up as a homosexual. One thing led to another and he was, in no time, derobbed as a pedophile. These were what love had done to him.

Cynthia only fared marginally better though she never went to any of those extremes. She finished from medical school to become that absent-minded doctor who will never trust any man. She very often misdiagnosed cases and prescribed wrong medications. She never talked to any of her colleagues and she did not have any close friends. She was however eventually helped to drop a little bit out of her woes when another doctor simply dropped out of the blues to strike up a relationship with her.

Just like Thomas, she could no longer trust any man and did not want any thing to do with them. Vengeance was beginning to creep into her mind, but then Thomas had remained her one and only true love and she did not quite want to let him go. As the new doctor dropped in, she was reluctant because her body could be there for him at the end, but her mind will never be his own. It looked like a confusing and complicated matter and that's why love has its own uncharted territory. It is not easy to understand it.

She had managed to hookup with her internist, Doctor Charles McDaniel. It took McDaniel almost six months to convince her to get closer to him despite her being his boss in the office and their living next doors to each other. He liked her because she was very plain and truthful. She liked him for the same characteristics and she did not want to disappoint him at the end and so she told him about Thomas. He refused to comment on Thomas. His reason was that any other man would have reacted that way. She was too pretty not to be able to elicit jealousy in any man. He only advised her to let bygones be bygones. She might forgive Thomas, but to forget him was out of the question.

As had been pointed out before, Cynthia was not exactly into Charles since her heart was still with Thomas, not minding what had happened. Charles on his own part was not fully into her. He was an extremely kind and compassionate man, and his love for her was born out of pity. He had known all along that there must have been something that happened to her in the past that must have led to that way of life.

He was of the expected opinion that Cynthia was too pretty to be left to pine away in misery and suffer in silence. He had come across such a case before, and that one was even worse.

He once had a close friend who was two years his senior in the secondary school. The boy was in his final year, which meant that he was about to be released into the real world. During their last four weeks vacation, he lived with his fiancée. She was working and so he lived in her house with her, and at times he would go with her to her work place.

There were no concrete plans, but they had agreed to get married as soon as he finished from school, which was going to be in about three months time. His heart was therefore now fully occupied with the idea of getting married very soon. While going back to school, she had bought all sorts of things for him, and since it was in February she also bought a valentine card to go with them. The card read: "You are my one and only sunshine, and should your light be extinguished, then I will surely go with you."

Two weeks after the resumption of school, he received a courier –delivered letter. Inside was a wedding invitation card. It was for the nuptials between Annabelle, his fiancée, and Amorata. He had come across Amorata on three different occasions in her house, and he was introduced to him as her cousin Jilto. He was, according to her, also her best friend's fiancée.

To add salt to injury, the card was posted on their wedding day, which meant that he received it three days after the wedding. He believed that it was a valentine joke and so he called her not to crack such jokes with him. He was shocked to learn in no uncertain way that she was actually married. She also warned him against making telephone calls to "this married woman."

Jacob, for that was his friend's name, was so broken hearted that his first reaction was to commit suicide. He had tried an overdose of a sleeping pill, but it turned out to be an analgesic, which therefore refused to send him to the other side. After this, he locked himself in his room as he went on hunger strike with the hope that he could die of starvation. A few days later, he was discovered unconscious in his room and they had to feed him intravenously to resuscitate him.

A couple of counseling sessions later, he agreed to live on and try to find another sunshine. He was however no longer his previous self. He was now, just like Cynthia, always absent-minded. Indeed he nearly failed his final examinations because of this. Even after that, he still found it impossible to get employment. Most employers found out that he was always absent minded even during interviews.

It was Charles McDaniel that called in the medics to take his friend to the hospital when he was unconscious. It was for this reason that when he came across Cynthia, he had to make moves to make sure that his boss did not have the same ultimate problem as his friend Jacob. Apart from that, she was very pretty.

THE REUNION

Love is longsuffering, and both Thomas and Cynthia have suffered for a long time, if that is what that statement is supposed to mean. Love never dies, and it was surely still there between both of them, not minding the fact that they had not seen each other for a long time. Unknown to either of them, fate was about to plot and weave one of those her intricate webs around them. They were to meet again and very soon too.

Cynthia had finally agreed to marry Charles but it was, as had been pointed out earlier, a half-hearted decision for she was still in love with Thomas.

On the eve of their wedding, they had accepted to go out with a few of their friends from work for a meal. "Restorante de Restaurant" was the talk of the town and that was where they went. It was a brand new place and it occupied the top floor of a twenty-one-story building. All the walls were of thick one-way tinted glasses and one could see the entire city while within it. It was the brainchild of their coworkers – the meal that is.

They all made it to the restaurant from work and they had each contributed for the occasion. While waiting to be served, they freely cracked jokes, and for the first time, some of them saw Cynthia laughing.

Cynthia suddenly stiffened, wide mouthed and looking straight ahead like one who had just seen a ghost. Everyone noticed that, and all began to look in that direction too. In fact she had just seen one, - it seemed to be a ghost from her past.

They both looked at each other, Cynthia and the ghost that is, and just as would be expected in dreams they kept looking at each other. The ghost had dropped the tray that he was carrying and their food poured on the floor while all the plates got broken. He did not seem to notice that. Everyone, customers and workers alike looked on with everyone wondering and puzzled at what it could have been that was going on. No one could figure out what was going on till Cynthia made her move. Charles was the only person in the entire hall who guessed what was going on.

Cynthia got up and began to take a couple of slow unsure steps towards the ghost, probably afraid, as she pointed out, that it might melt away like plasma which she suspected that it was. The ghost did the same with a few tottering steps as if it was learning to walk for the first time. Then just as if they heard the start whistle, they charged towards each other. They ran into each other's arms with each of them shedding enough tears to rinse off all their dinner plates.

Everyone clapped and applauded. The workers did so for their new colleague, Doctor Charles clapped for both of them because he was now sure that Cynthia had once again found where her heart was. As for the rest, they clapped because others were clapping. It was still a puzzle to them. A couple of the workers were busy shouting: *"Amore! Amore!! Amore!!!"* I am not too sure as to where they learnt that from, but they had probably watched too many non-English films.

Thomas sobbed uncontrollably while begging her for forgiveness. The tears that fell were mixed tears. Some were tears of happiness, some were tears of remorse and yet others were tears of uncertainty, but they were mainly tears of joy as he started:

O what a miserable man I have been
For my soul had long lingered in sadness
As my heart ached in my folly
O me miserum!

Your arrows have pierced my anguished heart
And its blood runs red all around.
I've always smelt the thought of you
That's more than the smell of a thousand roses.

Now as if leased anew my waning heart
A new life does come to it.
In distress I did weep before
Now that light from afar I do see.

When I pined in elusive joy
My heart did groan at the loss of you –
A loss triggered from my stupid folly.
Do return to me O my love.

Awake O my soul, awake and rejoice
For now aflight on the wings of love
Mine eyes do again your beauty behold.
Awake and rejoice O my soul.

Your face alone like hot knife to butter
Quickly melts my wants away –
A face that's so sweet and calm -
And here you pose like a dewy dawn.

You're more gracious than the weeping elm
Very early at the break of dawn.
Nothing like you have I ever seen,
Prior to now by these wearied eyes.

There you stand as in full repose –
A beauty never afore seen by man.
Your beauty beckons and it beckons to me,
For in your beauty resides my heart.

When you starred into my eyes,
My heart did skip like a maddened ball.
Very kind to my heart you've always been
In beauty that tickles and tickles my soul.

Thomas had hardly finished this poem of praise before he went on to apologize for all that he had done:

"Cynthia, please can you find a small space in your heart to forgive me. I have sinned against you and against God too, and I have abused as well as accused you falsely. I now realize that I was insane when I did what I did as well as when I said what I said."

"I thought I had lost you for ever Thomas."

"I thought so too, and I could not bear the thought of that."

"Thomas."

"Please forgive me."

"But it was all a misunderstanding and I forgave you a long time ago."

"Are you sure of that?"

"Yes, I am sure."

"No matter what, I still feel guilty."

"Feel guilty?"

"Yes."

"Why?"

"Because it was all my fault and one cannot change history."

"I am not trying to change any history."

"In that case, please still forgive me. When I saw you in that mans arms I simply lost my senses and mind as well as the power of reasoning. What I said was from the fact that I thought that what I saw was for real. I was afraid and enraged that I had lost you"

"I know that. You don't have to apologize."

"Please forgive me. I was blinded by love all through that time and I did not know what I was doing. It was as if an invisible Puppeteer was there pulling away at his strings to control me and my actions."

"What of me who did not try to contact you after that. I wanted to call you but I never came round to doing so. I have no idea why I never did that despite the fact that I itched to do so."

"It was the same with me, but most of the time I blamed myself so much for what had happened that I could not summon up enough courage to do so. I was too ashamed to face you."

"But I even wanted you the more after that. It took some time before it dawned on me that all it meant was that you loved me so much that you could go ballistics at what you saw. It meant that you could go mad at anyone or anything that will interfere with our relationship. It was surely unreasonable of me not to have made more concerted efforts to find you and win you back. Please forgive me too."

"If there is any forgiving to be done it has to be you forgiving me. After all it was me who started it all."

"Okay then. What of if we forgive each other together at the count of three."

"One, two three it is then."

"Who counts?"

"Me."

"Why."

"I guess that as the man, I am the head."

"Okay!"

"One, two, two and half, two and three quarters and THREE!"

"I forgive you!" They both chorused in unison just as if they had practiced that before now.

It had become the dawn of a new era of love between them, and with that he planted one of those Olympian kisses on her lips. It lasted quite some time, or at least so it seemed, and it could have set a new record regarding the length of time it took. In fact it will surely go into the Guinness book of records too. They seemed oblivious of all the people around who suddenly resumed their applause. This time around, it was for that kiss. As soon as they were able to disengage, Cynthia said:

"Please do not take this personally, but I could never have imagined that you could say all those things you said. That was the main reason that I did not take you all that serious then."

"I cannot even remember exactly what I said because I myself could not even believe that those things came from my own mouth. I was not the person saying them. The devil must have possessed me and said those things from within me without my realizing it. That was possible because love is blind."

"I doubt it. If love is blind how then did you see those things that you said that you saw?"

"The problem is that I saw only those things that I thought that I saw. I saw but I did not try to see. Love had struck me blind and I was like the blind man who while making a speech said, "I see." Whatever he has seen is in his imagination and he is just guessing."

"But that is not what they mean by that saying that love is blind."

"What do they mean then?"

"That it is blind to all ills and any wrongs from the other significant half and they will even be seen as good.

"I agree with you. It is also that it could blind the ability to reason, and that was the case with me."

"I see what you mean."

"I was so deeply in love with you that any thought of my loosing you, even if that is imagined, would be enough to bring out the beast in me."

"I was also madly in love with you. When McDaniel came along, that's my fiancée sitting over there I did not warm up to him, and intend to leave his story for a latter period. I only kept him at arms length while making it clear that he should know what he was getting into since you were still the custodian of my heart. My heart and thoughts will forever belong to you and you alone. The only thing that kept me going was the fact that I believed that God had planned it that way and that He had his own way of rewarding his servants."

"I was so devastated that I could not fit into anywhere, and that was why after a few total misadventures, I managed to turn up here as a banquet server, and on time too."

"In what way?" She interrupted.

"I only started here yesterday without realizing that it was that uncanny hand of fate that was weaving that her intricate web around me."

Incidentally it had been the same with me. Do you know that it was only today that our colleagues at work decided that we should come out for this meal? They claimed that it would be their final opportunity to see either of us single. I had always tried to delay the "D_DAY" because I was not exactly warmed up to him – Charles that is, though he was a very good man."

"I will never make this type of mistake again in my life. I can never afford to loose you again."

"Me too. I had always prayed that we should link up again, and the Lord had simply heard my prayers. May all glory and thanks be to Him! I had thought that He did not answer me, but now I know why it is said that Gods time is the best. He had just waited for the right moment.

Thomas was a changed man and all he wanted to do now was all he had in mind. He wanted to make an honest woman out of this already honest lady. There was no time to waste and as the very resourceful man that he was, he went into immediate action. He brought out his key ring from the pocket of his apron and started off sliding his keys out of them. People looked on without being able to figure out what he was up to. Only one person managed to think out aloud, and he was wrong by imagining that he was about to give her the duplicate keys to his apartment.

He then suddenly went down on one knee, and that was when it began to dawn on them. He presented the key ring to her with a request:

"Cynthia, will you marry me?"

The crowd, that now included the kitchen staff, did not wait for her to answer. They answered for her:

"Yes! Yes!! Yesss!!!"

Those words came, they echoed and they reverberated from every corner of the banquet hall. She immediately went down on her own knee to accept the invaluable engagement ring while shouting:

"O Yes, I will marry you!" This came with tears streaming down her lovely face. They were tears of absolute joy as they both jumped up only to find themselves in each other's arms. With their faces almost on each other's, she began to whisper the following words, which the muses had just put into her brain:

"Deep down in that darkness called my heart
I did grope within with some hopeless hope
Till you returned like early songs in me –
A subdued glow to light my soul.

"Like early birds my soul began to leap
As hopes of gladness return to me.
Amazed I stand and look at you –
A joyous marvel that the Lord had made.

"You've filled my heart with perfect light,
To turn my darkness into a joyous glow.
Your gentle words have stirred my soul
And pains of anger do flee from there.

"How I love you my lovely love
For my aches have eased at the sight of you.
Come to me my lovely love
For here we stand to part no more."

Cynthia had just finished pouring out her soul to him. Thomas was dumbfounded mainly because he could never have imagined that she was such a poet, but more importantly, he was too excited by what he heard to think clearly. But then the best was yet to come. Those muses had just inspired and composed an impromptu ODE TO TOM, which they left in her brain. She did not wait for Thomas to react before she started off once more:

"Your love is better than wine to me
O my fair and lovely Tom,
For like the roses amongst the harmful thorns
You stand amongst the rest to me.

"Your handsome face always comes to me,
Like the early songs of twitting birds.
Those dimples! O my God!!
Like the fragrance of jasmine they intoxicate my soul.

"Your hair like the darkest ebon
In tiny coiffeurs are set in honeycombs
To crown those eyes that ravish my heart –
O how 'am drunk in your lovely love.

"I am sore sick without your love,
So let me hear your voice again
Which always skips through my soul
Like reechoes of those heavenly lyres.

"Your voice often searches out at will
All those secret caverns of my innermost soul.
Do speak to me once again my love
That gladness might return to me.

"Oft as I lie asleep at night
Your face oftener wakes my heart.
Please do not always look at me
Since your face always consumes me like fire.

"Now that I always sleep and wake
Is it a waking sleep or what?
For my heart is always filled with thee
Since for you alone it is made to be.

"Come to me that we may for ever be
As two united in one as one;
For like the darkness to dewy dawns
Those woes will tend to flee from me."

"In truth I now know that love is not just long suffering, but it is also long lasting and unquenchable like an eternal light." Replied Thomas.

"Tell ne that which I don't know." She replied.

They then stood there silently, looked at each other, sized each other up and admired each other for a while before melting away. They were never seen again, neither in the hospital where Cynthia worked, nor in the restaurant where Thomas just began to work. None of their friends could tell what happened to them after that episode. It was only left to the imagination that they lived happily ever after.

As for Doctor Charles McDaniel, he was promoted to replace his former boss Cynthia when they could not hear from her. About four months later he married that one-eyed nurse that was his assistant. They also lived happily ever after.

Some people are often under such influence from fate that they always find themselves with certain similar situations. Doctor Charles McDaniel was a typical example of this. Rachael, the nurse that he got married to was not one-eyed from birth. He had suspected that because she occasionally seemed to be slightly aloof and she also showed trace signs of absent-mindedness.

Rachael was still fairly young when she got married to an older man. The man had assured her that he had spent all his life seeking his better half but he never found one until he came across her. He was handsome, articulate and funny as well as slightly wealthy. All these combined to help sweep Rachael off her feet. There was a twenty-year gap between their ages, but in the face of love, that was nothing. Anyway Judas, for that happened to have been his name, had never told her his actual age. He had adjusted it a little bit downwards.

One thing led to another and they were soon married in the Roman Catholic Church. Both of them belonged to this denomination. They lived in one city while her husband worked in another city that was some sixty miles away. He did not want to relocate there because he owned the house where they lived. Judas worked the night shift, which was from eight in the night to eight in the morning. Their arrangement was that since it would be risky for him to drive home each morning since he might be feeling sleepy, he had to come home at the end of his workweek instead. He worked for one week and then went off for one week. He claimed that for the week at work he might be sleeping in a friend's house.

This remained a very nice and convenient arrangement till her company sent her to evaluate some losses from a fire incident in the same city where her husband worked. She was an insurance evaluator. She joked about it with the lady that she met at the house because they bore the same surname. The fire had razed one wing of the house.

She had collected most of the data and information she needed when the lady's husband came home from shopping.

Lo and behold, it was her husband Judas. There will be no point trying to explain what followed. Suffice it to point out that the man checked out right away to allow the ladies sort it out and settle the issue by themselves. In this city, Jacob had wedded Mary his wife in the Anglican Church.

The older lady, Mary, had made up her mind that Rachael was a husband snatcher who was so bold as to invade her home as an insurance evaluator. Rachael was still too confused to have any opinions as to what was going on. Anyway she had to fight for her husband and so they managed to get into some physical explanations, if one can put it that way. Mary somehow managed to send a knitting pin flying towards Rachel. The dart made it straight into her left eye, and that was how she came to be the one-eyed Rachael.

After she recovered from the hospital, she decided to go into the nursing profession. This was because while on admission, the nurses were very good to her, very friendly and many sympathized with, and advised her. In order to console her, some even contributed money for her. She had lost both an eye and a husband! Jacob had abandoned her on the grounds that she had become a one-eyed ugly monster.

That was her story, and there was no way that it could not stir the compassionate heart of Doctor Charles McDaniel. And that was why they finally got hitched to each other.

It would not therefore be far fetched for one to see from all that had transpired and happened in the story between Cynthia and Thomas, as well as others, that love, as a phenomenon is an enigma.

In the annals of human endeavor man has, as had been pointed out earlier on, succeeded in conquering virtually every obstacle that had presented itself, except of course for love. Love seems to freely roam around unhindered and at will within its own familiar, common and surely ill understood and exclusive niche – Love's Uncharted territory.